"I'll fight you
every inch o[...]

Lorne damned [...]
stood facing ea[...]

A smile curled t[...]
mouth. "Has it not occurred to you
that if you were less reluctant, I might
soon tire of the game?"

Lorne's gaze flickered to the wide,
pavilioned, satin-covered bed. "You
know I'll never throw myself at you
like your other women. I'm not fooled
by your manly appearance or your
position of leadership. I see right
through you, my lord. I see a man
without honor!"

She knew she had hit a nerve, for his
eyes flashed with a deadly brilliance.
"So it is going to be a lengthy siege,
eh? We may become addicted to our
battles," he said, a note of warning in
his voice. "They may hold us together,
while your surrender might push us
apart. Will you risk it?"

Dear Reader,

This month we celebrate the publication of our 1000th Harlequin Presents. It is a special occasion for us, and one we would like to share with you.

Since its inception with three of our bestselling authors in May, 1973, Harlequin Presents has grown to become the most popular romance series in the world, featuring more than sixty internationally acclaimed authors. All of the authors appearing this month are well-known and loved. Some have been with us right from the start; others are newer, but each, in the tradition of Harlequin Presents, delivers the passionate exciting love stories our readers have come to expect.

We are proud of the trust you have placed in us over the years. It's part of the Harlequin dedication to supplying, contemporary fiction, rich in romance, exotic settings and happy endings.

We know you'll enjoy all of the selections in this very special month, and in the months to come.

Your friends at Harlequin

VIOLET WINSPEAR

a silken barbarity

Harlequin Books

TORONTO • NEW YORK • LONDON
AMSTERDAM • PARIS • SYDNEY • HAMBURG
STOCKHOLM • ATHENS • TOKYO • MILAN

In life you can have only one great love.

The Koran

Harlequin Presents first edition August 1987
ISBN 0-373-11006-5

CHAPTER ONE

IT WAS A DAY OF SAVAGE HEAT, and then came the storm, a cloud of sulfurous dust that covered the sun. The dust storm raged all night, and by dawn the orange and date groves were devastated. The long shutters were torn from the plantation house, lamps and vases had crashed to the floor and a flood of water had broken in from the irrigation tower.

Lorne stood on the gallery and felt forlorn beyond tears. They would have helped as she gazed down at the water puddling the hall and heard intermittent sirens of wind breaking the hush that had followed the nightlong frenzy of the sirocco. That soulless wind that brought disaster in its wake ... so it was said.

It had followed upon days of heat beneath leaden skies, turning the desert into an ominous landscape. Even yet the heat seemed to sear the walls of the battered house, and Lorne could feel moisture creeping down her back. Her shirt, pulled out from the band of her skirt, clung to her skin, and her moist hands clung to the gallery rail.

In furious gusts the wind had broken over the outside veranda, forcing gritty dust and flies into the paneled rooms. Now it smothered every surface of the French furniture and hung in the air like a miasma.

With her courage almost as battered as the house, Lorne leaned against the balustrade, her mouth dry, her eyes smarting, her spirit whipped like the date palms in the groves. An unhinged shutter kept rattling—it was as if something alien was trying to get at her, each creak and bang flaying her nerves. She was drained of the energy required to go and close the shutter.

Tense as a cat with no place to hide, she tried in vain not to think of the silent figure laid out on the bed in the master bedroom. She shivered in the heat, the striking blue of her eyes shadowed by the events of the night. A blue that could be likened to that in chapel windows.

There had been a chapel attached to the convent school where she had spent her childhood, and where her Desirée instincts had often rebelled against the discipline and the dormitory, where privacy was an unknown factor and the food so often plain and tasteless. The good Sisters decreed that the flesh be subdued to the spirit, which meant that the classrooms were chilly even when a few rays of sunlight came stealing through the trees in the cloistered garden.

Then on her seventeenth birthday, quite out of the blue, she had been called into Sister Superior's office and told that she was to go and live with her grandfather. Up until that time Lionel Desirée had ignored her existence, but from the moment Lorne arrived at L'Oasis she felt as if she had found a home she could love. A fascinating home set among the shady groves of fruit, where the constant trickling of water in the irrigation ditches made even the hottest time of the day seem cool. At night she would lie in bed and listen to the friendly croaking of frogs.

She had been captivated by the desert, and riding there at dawn, or when the great stars clustered in the evening sky, had been a joy that had never palled.

Now she stood alone and afraid on the wide-timbered gallery overlooking the hall. Alone because yesterday the servants had fled. Superstitious *fellahin*, who had taken fright not only from the mounting sandstorm but also because the Old Lion lay dead in the house.

The manservant Sadik had been the last to leave, his conscience smitten by the sight of Lorne at the bedside of the lifeless giant of a man whom she had grown to love in the two years she had lived at L'Oasis. She had grown accustomed to his gruff arrogance and had learned to accept his unforgiving attitude to her mother, whom he had never forgiven for marrying an Englishman.

Suddenly in the bedroom with the tall rosewood doors something crashed to the floor, and Lorne's tenuous hold on her courage was almost shattered. She wanted to run to the stables and throw herself across the back of Firefly, but it seemed such a heartless thing to do, to ride off and leave her grandfather alone in the storm-torn house. He had cared for her in his way, treating her, it was true, more like a boy than a girl.

Her lips moved, and she found she was murmuring one of the prayers that the Sisters at the convent school had made their pupils intone morning and evening. But prayer didn't blot from her mind the convulsed look on her grandfather's face and the way he had lurched into his room, crying out something as he fell across the bed. No amount of shaking or pleading had awoken him from his seizure, and finally she had covered his distorted face with the sheet.

Bleakly she gazed down into the hall. Her thick, light blond hair swung away from her cheekbone as she leaned over the balustrade and strained her ears to catch a sound that seemed unrelated to the wind. A clatter of hooves on stone, a jingle of a bridle, which made her wonder if one of the servants had returned.

Even as she hoped for this, an instinctive touch of fear made her retreat from the staircase. A shadow had moved down there, a tall, cloaked figure that moved deliberately into view. The cloak wrapped his figure from neck to booted heel, and Lorne found herself locking eyes with him as he placed a boot upon the bottom tread of the staircase.

"W-what do you want—how dare you come in here!" Her words came in a nervous rush, and in her agitation she spoke in English. "Y-you have no right to come into this house—"

"You would be astonished by the extent of my rights." His voice was deep, his formation of English vowels striking oddly against Lorne's ears. Then all at once she recognized him.... She had seen this man one evening in this house. She had just come in from a ride and was about to enter her grandfather's study when raised, almost savage voices had made her retreat across the hall. From there she had watched this man stride from the house with rage written all over him. Later on at dinner she had been told by Lionel Desirée not to ask questions. His business with Razul al Kebîr Bey was nothing to do with her. She was to forget his existence.

"He won't come here again," Lion assured her. "He's proud as the deuce, and he abominates the fact that my plantation is built on his territory, as he calls it. I had written permission from the old *cadi* himself. The high and mighty Razul Bey is but a nephew who snatched the power when the time came...."

"It is being said in Bar-Soudi that your grandfather has died."

Again that imperious voice struck against Lorne's raw-edged nerves, and when the owner of it began to mount the stairs in an intentional way, she wheeled toward the bedroom where Lionel Desirée lay dead.

All she could think of was the enmity that had existed between the two men, and there was a pistol in Lion's room. Hurriedly she wrenched open the rosewood doors and raced across the room, and every nerve in her body was aware that the figure in the rust-colored cloak was pursuing her. For some unbridled reason she had an image of that cloak being flung over her head, and with a shaking hand she pulled open the bureau drawer and clutched hold of the gun. She flung round and stared at Razul Bey in the doorway.

"Put down the weapon." There was curtness and a hint of mockery in his voice. "I have come to L'Oasis to assist you."

"Assist *me*?" Scornfully she leveled the pistol at his chest. "I happen to know how things stood between you and my grandfather. I'm a Desirée, as well, and I'm aware that when one of your people hates, he includes every member of the family."

"*La justice du bey.*" Even as he spoke the words, Razul Bey took a stride toward her. "I don't come here in a mood of benevolence, but be assured that I have my reason for being here."

"To enjoy the fact that Lion is dead?" Lorne looked him straight in the eyes. "He told me how much you hated it that L'Oasis stands on land that you say is yours. If you've come here to throw me off my grandfather's property, then you can think again!"

Lorne's eyes burned a deep blue as she swept the tousled hair back off her brow. If she had to shoot this man, then she wanted to shoot straight, in the way Lion had taught her. Never before had she felt such animal tension—her body shook with it as she faced Razul Bey. From head to heel he was alien to her—almost barbaric in looks and posture.

In her two years at L'Oasis she had learned something of the people. She knew they took their vendettas with a deadly seriousness. Family feuds were carried on from one generation to the next.

"I am not about to argue the finer points of land ownership with a bit of a girl." His very stance seemed to signify threat as he looked her up and down. "I am warning you that if you don't lay down the weapon, then I shall be forced to make you do so."

His imperious look and his menacing tone of voice were so infuriating that Lorne forgot to be afraid of her own vulnerability, here in this plantation house, which the sand-storm had almost wrecked.

"Get out of my grandfather's house." She hoped that some of Lion's harsh pride rang in her voice. "Go on, get out!"

"Shall I," he said, almost softly, "tell you about your grandfather, this man you venerate, with whose dead body you kept vigil all through the storm?"

"W-what is there to tell?"

"Perhaps enough to make you hate him."

"I could never do any such thing." The very thought swayed her back on her heels, and the pistol wavered in her hand, making him narrow his eyes in the lean, sun-darkened face, which was surmounted by a head robe bound with the gleaming gold and scarlet cords of his high standing in the region. If there was something ludicrous in the stand she was taking, she was too emotional right now to realize it.

Lion lay dead. She had no one to care about her anymore. And he had cared despite the inferences this man was making.

"I won't listen to your lies!"

"Lies don't happen to pass my lips," he rejoined. "If Lionel Desirée led you to believe that he brought you to L'Oasis out of love and concern for you, then he was the liar."

"He did love me." As she made her protest, she loathed the man who stood before her. "How would you know otherwise?"

"I do know."

Lorne couldn't take her eyes from his adamant face, like some golden sculpture, shaded beneath the cheekbones and in the clefting of his chin.

"And I think you should know," he said deliberately. "Lionel Desirée was so determined to remain at L'Oasis that when the lease on the land ran out two years ago, he offered me his virginal granddaughter in exchange. She was but a schoolgirl, he told me, guarded by nuns at a convent. She was untouched, pure as the snow on the Atlas mountains, the kind of girl to be worth a bag of gold in the marketplaces where the sale of women still goes on. Forbidden places in the heart of the desert, where your revered Lion would have put you on display rather than be parted from the one thing in his life that meant something to him—this house and those fruit groves surrounding it, which the wind has torn to shreds."

He paused, as if to let his words sink into Lorne's mind. He held her gaze with eyes that drilled his incredible words into her head.

She gazed back at him aghast. "How incredibly wicked of you to say such things—"

"The wickedness isn't mine, mamzelle." Razul Bey spoke with a curl to his lip, and then he sprang, as dangerously agile as any sand cat, and her wrist was gripped in merciless fingers, which forced her to release the pistol. It clattered to the floor, and he kicked it out of reach with his boot. A cry involuntarily escaped Lorne as she found herself in his clutches. She felt his touch right through the thin material of her shirt, and her body shrank with dismay at finding itself so close to his alien figure, enwrapped in the cloak to which clung an aromatic smoke that was almost drugging.

"You damn brute!" She struggled furiously but was no match for a man as strong as this one. "You liar! Take your hands off me!"

Instead he marched her out of Lion's room, on to the gallery. "You need boots and a cloak and, by Allah, if you don't stop resisting me, then I shall quieten you with my hand. Which room is yours?"

"D-don't manhandle me!" Lorne had never found herself in such a predicament before, and there was no one to help her. She could scream this house down and there was no one to hear. Then a cry escaped her as he shook her into submission.

"Hysterical females try my patience to the limit. Come to your senses before I'm obliged to knock some reasoning into you. L'Oasis was lashed by the tail of the storm last night, and the storm isn't over yet. It will turn upon itself and will come this way again. Hasn't one night of it been enough for you, or do you want more of the same, in a house with a dead body?''

"You'll say anything—do anything to get me out of it." She flung him a look of venom and hated the fear that welled up inside her when she met his eyes. Amber-colored eyes beneath a pair of barbarously black brows.

"Which room is yours?" he rapped.

With resentment and reluctance she indicated a door farther along the gallery. She was marched into her bedroom, and Razul Bey stood over her while she stamped her feet into riding boots, then adjusted the cloak she wore when she rode in the desert.

"Are you taking me to Bar-Soudi?"

"Is that where you wish to go?"

She nodded assent and saw him react with a slightly dismissive shrug of his shoulders. She turned to pick up her riding crop, which lay on the table where the kerosene lamp still flickered its flame. It had burned through the night, a token of comfort as the wind howled and the house shook. Now, as Lorne picked up the crop, she thought of a passage in a book she had been reading, about a pagan funeral that two young soldiers had arranged for their brother when he was killed in battle.

Lorne swung the crop, and the kerosene lamp was swept from the table, spilling oil and flame upon the timber floor. The flames leaped instantly, fed by the wind through a broken shutter, bright and hot, reaching for her even as an arm hooked itself about her waist and swept her out on to the gallery.

"You did that purposely!" The eyes looking down at her were as scorching as the fire taking hold in her bedroom.

"Yes." She gave him a challenging, willful look. "Lion will appreciate his pagan funeral and the fact that all you'll have left of L'Oasis will be a pile of ashes. Only one thing is missing, and that's the dog at his feet—it should be you!''

For a long moment, as the flames leaped higher and consumed the muslin curtains around her bed, Razul Bey seemed to have an almost detached look in his eyes, as if his control over his emotions was as resolute as hers was capricious.

There was no sign of anger, yet Lorne felt sure that her remark had bitten into him. The fire was crackling and spitting its sparks at them as it reached the bedroom door.

"Come!" He hurried her down the stairs, for soon the fire would spread. The bulk of the plantation house was timbered, and it wouldn't take long for the flames to consume the property, but Lorne felt not a tinge of regret for the compulsion that had overtaken her. Forgotten were the restraints the nuns had imposed upon her from a young age. All that mattered was that she take a swipe at the cruel and outrageous lies that this man had uttered.

Hadn't Lion told her that men of the Near East were no more to be trusted than pitching your tent in the shade of rocks, where a sand cat might be hiding?

Outside in the fitful daylight the wind lashed at the palm trees in the forecourt of the house, bending them back and forth as if to split them apart. Lorne drew the cowl of her cloak over her head, bending her body to the force of the grit-laden wind as she followed Razul Bey to where a group of men in robes were crouched beside the shielding humps of their camels. When Lorne realized that she was expected to ride one of these creatures that in a sandstorm could close its nostrils against the driving dust, she shouted above the wind that she wanted to go on horseback to Bar-Soudi. She was turning toward the stables when a hand descended upon her shoulder.

"Your horses bolted in the night."

"Firefly—he's gone?" The hot tears welled into her eyes, and she could hardly bear this further loss. Heatedly she swung to face the bey. "Are you telling some more lies? Did you let the horses loose in your godforsaken desert—oh, I wouldn't put it past you!"

"In their fear of the storm, they kicked their way out of the stalls," he replied. "They won't run loose for long. They will find a master."

Somehow the word made her flinch. *None of this can be happening,* she thought. *I shall wake up in a minute and find it's all been a nightmare.*

A sudden gush of flame swept back and forth from one of the upper windows of the plantation house, and at a curt word of command from Razul Bey, his retinue of men leaped to their feet. In a kind of daze Lorne was led to one of the tawny-red camels, still in its kneeling position so she could climb into the saddle, every inch of her shrinking against the pommel when the bey climbed in behind her.

As the camel reared to its feet, the rest followed suit and, with loping strides, rode in a line through the gates of L'Oasis, past the wreckage of the groves, toward the desert.

"Now we ride like the wind itself." The bey's voice struck through the whine of the sand-filled air. He spoke those words in English, but when he turned his head to give an order to his men, he spoke in his own language.

It was a language Lorne hadn't mastered during her stay at her grandfather's house. He hadn't encouraged the use of the barbaric-sounding words, applying himself to correcting her French until it was almost as good as his own. Then he would say to her: "Now you are a Frenchwoman, such as your mother was until she became besotted by a blond English sahib!"

In time she had forgiven him for his scorn of her father. Much like Razul Kebîr, Lion had been tough and tyrannical, believing in his own invincibility, and heedless of the desires of other people. Such men rarely asked for pity, or

gave it, and with her head bowed in its cowl, Lorne visual-
ized the burning house, soon to be her grandfather's pyre.

She wanted to give way to her tears, but she was too aware
of the proximity of Razul Bey. The lurch and sway of the
camel made their bodies come into contact, and whenever
this happened she cringed, thought of the things he had said
and wanted this ride over and done with.

Soon, she told herself, the flat-roofed houses of Bar-Soudi
would be glimpsed through the swirling dust, and she would
be free of the man.

There was no doubt in her mind that he meant to leave her
at the Hotel Ramis. She had no money with her, but she
knew that her grandfather's account was in the local bank.
She hoped she would have access to the account, as Lion's
sole beneficiary, and it made the day seem less doomed that
in a matter of hours she would be among the European
tourists staying at the hotel.

Lorne welcomed the thought, for these men who surrounded her on the loping camels were as enigmatic as the
desert itself. She could hardly bear the man who sat so un-
bearably close to her, but there was nothing she could do—
she had to endure him until they reached Bar-Soudi.

CHAPTER TWO

LORNE AWOKE SUDDENLY, a girl whose emotions had been stretched on a rack over the preceding hours, who dazedly realized that the swaying gait of the camel had rocked her off to sleep in the saddle. She didn't know for how long. Perhaps for moments only—or had it been for hours?

The string of camels were proceeding along a stony pathway that gradually went uphill, until high walls and a battlemented gateway confronted them. There were stone towers at either side of the gates, swung open by men in uniform.

Guards? Lorne peered through the mist of dust that was swirling about in the air, musky and stinging. There were no guards at Bar-Soudi. It was a town where the inhabitants and the visitors went about freely.

Oh God, where on earth was she?

Her frightened but silent cry must have transmitted itself to the man who, in guiding the camel, held his arms in a kind of snare around her figure.

"This is El Karah," he said. "We are entering the courtyard of my palace—"

"Your—what?" she exclaimed. She was still a little sleep-dazed and inclined to wonder if she was dreaming this enormity. "You can't be serious?"

"I will allow that the palace always looks better in sunlight." His voice above her head was totally impersonal, as if he were a guide and she a tourist. "Its architecture is somewhat obscured at the moment, but it is, in my opinion, one of the finest examples of workmanship in the land. It was built by an ancestor of mine upon the ruins where many armies clashed and died, each one as convinced as the other that their banner of faith was the better one. There are chambers still intact beneath the palace, where prisoners were ... encouraged to change their minds."

"I don't care what's in, around and under your palace," Lorne said furiously, her body twisted around in the saddle so she could hurl the words in his face. "You led me to believe that you were taking me to Bar-Soudi—it's infamous of you to bring me here! This is the last place on earth I want to be—do you hear me?"

"With clarity, *mon enfant*."

"I'm not your child," she stormed. "I'm not anything to you, nor would I ever want to be! I want to be taken to the Hotel Ramis. I demand to be taken there!"

"You demand?" A smile touched his mouth, but it wasn't one of amusement. "You are indeed a rib of the old man Desirée. He, too, was full of his own demands."

"Shut up, and turn this camel around," she said hotly.

His eyes narrowed at her tone of voice, but before the black lashes screened them, Lorne caught the tigerish gleam in those amber-colored eyes. Even as she felt the rising power of the sirocco, lashing again at everything in its path, she felt the power of this man who governed El Karah. A man to whom a woman could mean less than a hawk on his wrist or a stallion trained to his every command.

The authority of his position was stamped into his features, and Lorne realized that anything could be hiding behind those hooded eyelids. Dangers she had barely thought about, even when she rode alone in the desert.

"There is another historical feature in El Karah." He softly drawled the words. "The old slave market, with a platform of rough-hewn stone upon which the slaves were set up for sale. Men rode in from the hill country to view the merchandise, and those who fetched the highest prices were the vigorous young boys and the virginal girls.''

He paused, and the wind howled across the vastness of the courtyard and through fretted archways into the inner court of the palace. The camels had come to a standstill, and the bey's tribesmen awaited his command to dismount. Lorne felt the tumultuous beating of her heart as Razul Bey leaned closer to her and captured her gaze with his smoky-gold eyes.

She had heard it said that time stood still in the desert, and that in certain ways its people and customs stayed as they had been for countless years.

She could believe it when she looked at the bey of Karah. She realized with a frightened thump of her heart that had she submitted quietly to his initial offer of assistance, she might now be safe at the hotel in Bar-Soudi. His cultured side had been in control of him, until her own impetuous action in setting fire to the plantation house.

Now the barbaric side of his nature had taken charge of his actions, and Lorne had to find a way to reason with him. Pleading words would have mortified her; she couldn't beg of him to take her to Bar-Soudi, and he was so much richer than she that to offer money would have been absurd, especially when the money came from Lion's estate.

"People in Bar-Soudi will wonder what has become of me," she said. "The authorities will charge you with abduction, if you keep me here."

"The authorities will probably assume that you perished in the fire with Lionel Desirée." His voice held a silken note of mockery. "You applied the flame, but they will come to the assumption that the kerosene lamp was flung from the table in a burst of wind."

"Y-your men know that you've brought me here—" Lorne struggled to hide the panic that his words ignited in her.

"My men are bound by loyalties you would have no conception of." Now his eyes were mocking her. "They are desert born; you are but a piece of sugar in the mouth of Kismet."

Lorne caught her breath, swept by a sinking feeling as he gave the signal for his camel to kneel. As it settled itself with a jingling of accoutrements, Razul Bey alighted and reached for Lorne. She clung to the pommel as if it were her only safeguard, and he laughed, and she heard an echo of that laughter among his men. She felt the reddening of her wind-stung cheeks. A piece of sugar, he had called her, as if here in El Karah she could be hidden away by him, treated in any way he wished, her rights swept away by the sandstorm.

"T-this has gone far enough," she said. "You've had your little joke, Razul Bey. You've paid me back f-for what I did—"

"Do you really imagine that any joke was intended?" Forcibly he lifted her out of the saddle. "No one, mamzelle, calls me a dog without paying for the insult. No woman calls me a liar without learning a few painful truths. No one in the city of El Karah will turn a hair that I bring a woman to my *serai*, even though her hair happens to be foreign gold."

Lorne stared up at him through the dusty veil that the winds had flung over the sky. His animal stillness, her sense of peril, both were allied to the dangerous mood of the sirocco, still flaying skin and nerves as it turned day into dusk.

There was something fatal and forbidding in the air, as if some part of Lorne was inclined to believe that what was happening was written in the churning sands.

Oh, but that was superstitious nonsense. She forced it out of her mind and pushed the cowl away from her face. "You're in a position of authority." Once again she had to try to reason with Razul Kebîr. "How can you behave in such an unprincipled way, and then assume the right to punish other men when they do wrong? By bringing me here—by forcing me to stay, you're committing a crime, and you know it."

She drew a deep breath in the hope of calming her voice. "You'll be found out!"

"There is always a chance of that." His shoulders lifted the great cloak in a fatalistic shrug. "But by then, *mon enfant*, you will have learned a lesson which your grandfather failed to teach you. He encouraged you to have the tongue of a stablehand, yet at the same time he said of you, *elle a le coeur pur*. We shall see. You have already shown the willful side of yourself—I may also discover that your so-called purity of person is but a piece of glass, posing as a jewel."

"We-ll, of all the—you boor!" Lorne broke into a stormy flood of words, swept from the path of reason by the temper he aroused in her. "You have the manners and the behavior of a road sweep! Some gentleman of the desert! The insignia you wear so arrogantly is nothing but fake!"

Again he shrugged, as if her words did no more than brush his skin like the wings of flies in the hot sky. "It is said that we are a reflection of the company we keep, so why should I play the gentleman with someone who behaves like an arsonist instead of a lady?"

"So that's your excuse for your behavior?" Lorne flung back her hair in a gesture of defiance, the deep natural wave made limp by the sultriness in the air. "I can see that it means nothing to you that I went through a hellish night— you want to add to the hell I've been through."

"I intend," he said deliberately, "to teach one member of the Desirée family that here in the desert I am the superior being. Like most women of the West you want a world in which there is no difference between men and women. You need to be taught that there is an infinity of difference."

"And you are the man to do it?" She poured scorn upon his words, even as she felt herself shaking like the palm leaves had shaken in the storm. Her fingers clenched. She wanted her riding crop in her grip so she could slash at his face with it. She wanted to go down fighting him with more than words. He had an answer for everything. He was totally unmoved by her grief at losing her grandfather—he was pleased that Lion was gone so he could take back his precious piece of land.

"You ice-blooded brute!" she flung at him. "You've got your land, so why can't you leave me alone?"

"Are you so afraid of my intentions?" He smiled, but it was a smile that left his eyes as amber-hard as those of a tiger.

"You don't frighten me—" Even as she spoke, he closed strong hands upon her waist. She was swung clear off the ground, and kicking, struggling, calling upon all the cuss words she had ever found in books, Lorne was carried across a small tiled court, which was separate from the main apartments of the palace. A fountain splashed into a pool, as in the arms of Razul Bey she made her undignified entrance into a room that was wide and cool, with a fretwork archway to which she clung in an effort to restrain a man whose arms and shoulders were strapped with muscle.

"Let go!" he rapped.

Seething with fury and a definite streak of fear, Lorne relaxed her grip. Right now her efforts to escape him were useless. Her struggles merely emphasized his superior strength.

She was dropped to her feet beneath a large half-moon window filled in with an intricate carving of wood in place of glass. Beneath the window there was an enormous couch of the same crescent shape. "Sit down." It needed but a slight push, and she found herself tumbling among the cushions. "I shall order breakfast, and you will eat with me. I don't imagine that food has entered your mouth in the past twenty-four hours—unless you are contemplating a refusal to eat?"

"Will you force-feed me?" she asked bitterly. "The way you've forced me into your palace?"

She glanced around her at the dark wood furniture with opulent inlays of lighter woods. Underfoot there were rugs that glimmered with a thousand colors. The glow of silk-shaded lamps dispelled the murky daylight, revealing tap-estried walls and a ceiling painted with figures in gauzy draperies, in reclining attitudes around a lotus-shaped pool.

"This place—what is it?" A suspicion daggered her mind even as the words escaped from her lips.

"The *serai*," he replied, and his eyes were fixed upon her as he untied his cloak and flung it aside, to reveal a jerkin of finely woven strands of leather and breeches that were gathered into knee-high leather boots.

"What is a—*serai*?" She had to hear him say it—she had to have it spelled out, so there would be no doubt in her mind that every inch of him was as despicable as the things he had said about her grandfather, there in the very room where Lion lay dead.

"The portion of my palace reserved for my women." As he spoke, he took a cheroot from a box of hammered silver and placed it between his lips. He applied a flame, which played over his features before he closed the lighter. His forehead, nose and jawline were faultlessly structured, yet to call him handsome would have been a misnomer. Hand-some men had a certain charm, even a theatrical appeal— this man was formidable, and his prolonged gaze brought the color rushing into Lorne's face.

"You boor!" Words came alive on her lips again. Shock and fear were replaced by the most flaming anger she had ever felt in her life. "You desert hoodlum—how dare you bring me to this—this slave house?"

His lips smiled slowly around the cheroot. Smoke trav-eled toward her, bringing the aroma that had mingled with the smell of leather and horse on his cloak. He was vivid, arrogant, compelling in his desert clothes. He was a law unto himself in this part of the world, and he knew it.

Lorne's fingers clenched a cushion, which, unaware, she had drawn toward her. A pathetic protection, she realized, against the intentions he might have in mind. She wildly searched his amber eyes—amber, believed by Near Easterns to be the soul of the tiger. It entered her head that in every way he had the animal power and grace that took no heed of anything but its own satisfaction.

As smoke wreathed his robed head, he gazed around the exotic room, where everything was designed for comfort and pleasure. His gaze lifted lazily to the ceiling, and he contemplated the group of *houris* around the lotus pool, looking as if they awaited the imperious call to the master's couch.

Lorne's fingernails were in danger of ripping the satin cushion to threads as Razul Bey returned his gaze to her face. He said not a word. He left her in torment with her thoughts.

"You have a—a piece of stone for a heart." She had wanted to say it with scorn, but the words came huskily from her dry lips. She felt a wave of weakness, and the last thing she wanted was to fall in a heap at the booted feet of Razul Kebîr. With an effort she unfastened her cloak in order to feel less burdened. She felt as if she were being spun around like a toy in a careless hand as she pushed the cloak wearily from her shoulders.

White-robed servants entered the room, and with polite *salaams* they took their orders from the bey. He spoke in the deep-throated language that meant nothing to Lorne, and all she could hope was that he had ordered coffee. Her throat was parched. She was dying for a coffee, but she certainly wasn't going to ask for anything, except her release from this—prison.

When the servants departed to carry out his orders, Razul Bey lowered himself to the couch, looking totally indifferent when she drew herself as far away from him as possible.

His every move set her pulses hammering, but he seemed as detached from her feelings as if they were nonexistent. And she imagined they were, for a man reared in the belief that women were only ornamental, put on earth to give pleasure and provide children, preferably sons because they enhanced the father's self-esteem.

Lorne called upon all her self-reliance, for like the fire she had started, things had got out of her control, and she didn't know whether to scream, run or leap out of her skin at the slightest shift of Razul Bey's powerful body. Try as she might, she couldn't deny the possibility that her disappearance would be blamed on the fire. The timbered house had stood a long time in the hot sunlight, which had dried out every beam and joist, every window frame and door. It would roast in the blaze, and there wouldn't be too much curiosity if there were no remains to substantiate her demise. The house servants would be questioned, and they'd confirm that she had been alone with the dead body of her grandfather.

She pushed tiredly at her tousled hair. Tears threatened, but she was determined not to cry in front of Razul Bey. Where she was concerned, there wasn't a bone of compassion in him.

"I can't—" Lorne's voice was so husky as to be almost inaudible. "I can't begin to understand why you've brought me here. Surely you'd prefer to see the back of me?"

"Au contraire." He lounged against the cushions, and there emanated from him a potent aura of masculinity, especially so in this room designed to enhance the charms of a kept woman. "Those lips of yours might spill with venom rather than honey, but to look upon, they are most inviting. Though your hair, at the moment, is a mass of tangles, when attended to, it is gold shaded like the desert dunes where I often ride. Your eyes, *ma femme*, are the color of

wild irises, and when the sand dust is washed from your skin, it promises to be very touchable.''

As his words filtered through her mind, Lorne felt a jangling sense of alarm—a very personal sort of alarm. Life, until this morning, hadn't taught her that there were men such as Razul Bey. Seeing him in her grandfather's house hadn't warned her that their paths would cross in this fashion. Straight from convent school she had gone to live at L'Oasis, in some ways as isolated as the school had been....

Now, in one awful swoop, she found herself with a man who looked as dangerous as a dozen other men put together.

She half raised a hand, as if to appeal to his better nature. Was it what he really wanted, to see her groveling to him? Did he say such suggestive things just to frighten her? It had to be so. He was foreign to her, and they were alien to each other—nothing else could truly be intended.

As she sat there, racked by uncertainty, the servants entered the room, carrying trays of food. A gleaming, long-spouted pot, cream jug and cups were placed on the ebony table in front of the curving couch. Domed dishes and plates were set in readiness, but it was the rich aroma of the coffee that interested Lorne. More than ever she was longing for a cup.

She raised it eagerly to her lips and drank thirstily, not minding that it was strong and subtly flavored, for that was how Lion had liked his coffee.

"Now do you feel like eating some food?" Lean fingers lifted the domed lids to reveal succulent rissoles accompanied by a side helping of fried kidneys and tomatoes.

At the smell of the food, Lorne felt helpless to refuse. There was nothing to be gained in adding to her feeling of weakness. In fact, it looked as if she was going to need every ounce of her strength in dealing with Razul Kebîr.

She helped herself to the food and accepted one of the sesame rolls, which were warm to the touch. Once she started to eat, she couldn't stop, her eyes fixed on her plate as she tried to be unaware of her table companion. A hopeless quest, for he imposed his every movement and glance upon her, possibly without even trying.

"You must have another of these." He placed another rissole upon her plate and added some more halves of deliciously sweet tomato. "It is quite obvious that you have not eaten for many hours."

"Sorry to be making a pig of myself," she said tensely. "I'm not usually such a glutton, but yesterday I didn't feel like eating. I don't expect you to appreciate my feelings, not where my grandfather's concerned. You hated him, but I didn't. Y-you wouldn't have said those awful things about him, had you really known him."

A silence hung over the table, then a brown hand lifted the coffeepot and replenished her cup. "I really wish you could remain so innocent, but if I allowed your illusions I should be left with the label of liar hung around my neck."

Lorne flashed a look at him. "Those horrible things you said—they have to be a pack of lies! As if my very own grandfather—as if he'd offer me to a—stranger!"

"An alien such as I?" Razul Bey's amber eyes were fixed hard upon her face. "You retain the naïveté of your upbringing, *mon enfant*. You have no awareness of how ruthless some men can be in the pursuit of what they desire. Lionel Desirée had but one desire, and today you burned it to the ground."

Lorne turned away from his unfeeling gaze. It was beyond belief that Lion had sent for her in order to appease this barbaric-looking man. It didn't bear thinking about . . . yet she had heard that here in the desert it was no unusual thing for a woman to be exchanged for a racing camel or a handful of sheep. Her fingernails ripped the surface of the satin cushion as she wondered what it was her grandfather had cried out just before he died.

A shudder swept Lorne as she remembered the look on his face. He had wanted to go on living at L'Oasis, and he could well have been a man who died with something awful on his conscience. Something he had wanted to say in those terrible seconds before he collapsed.

"Y-you didn't have to tell me." Lorne spoke in a strained voice. "It was brutal of you to—to even imply that some sort of a bargain was struck between you. But now I realize why you brought me here."

"I wonder if you do fully realize?" As he leaned toward her, Lorne reached for a weapon of defense. Not much of a weapon, but it would serve to show him the depth of her contempt, and quite deliberately, she struck him across the face with the spray of jasmine that one of the servants had placed on the table. There was a splatter of star-shaped petals, and then the sound of Razul Bey's softly mocking laughter.

"What a pity for you," he drawled, "that, unlike the rose, the jasmine flower has no thorns."

"What a pity I didn't put a bullet through you!"

For a moment longer he smiled, then his fingers gripped her chin, and he placed an insistent kiss upon her mouth. She held her breath through the kissing, as if that would make her as unfeeling as a statue, a block of ice that couldn't feel his lips burning against hers.

"Now, perhaps, you realize," he murmured.

"Yes, my Lord Razul, that you are even more despicable than I had supposed."

His mouth hardened, and his look of sensuality was gone. He raked over her a look of casual arrogance. "Did I liken you to a piece of sugar in the mouth of Kismet? I should have said a spoonful of bitter aloes."

"I hope you can bear a bitter taste in your mouth, my lord?"

"Indeed so." His eyes dwelt upon the scornful set of her lips. "But if not, I can always exchange you for a camel."

Suddenly she had no ready answer to his taunt. Inside herself she felt shattered—miserably betrayed by the fate that had brought her to the desert in the first place. Fate—Kismet—the people of the East believed in it without question.

She glowered at him from behind her lashes. "Go to blazes!"

He inclined his robed head, then rose to his feet with a supple movement of a body in perfect condition. "I shall leave you to become accustomed to your new quarters. Through the beaded curtain, there are other rooms, so make yourself at home in the *serai*."

"My prison!" she flung at his back.

Razul Kebîr didn't bother to contradict her.

CHAPTER THREE

LORNE GLANCED DESPAIRINGLY around the room, an odd feeling sweeping over her, a sense of something happening as it had happened before. The bead curtain stirred, then the tapering beads were still again. She shivered and hugged herself, while the reality of all this sank into her mind.

This was no figment of a dream—it was too horribly real, that she had been brought here on the saddlebow of a camel. The image of her abductor was stamped on her brain, as imposing as he was arrogant, as threatening as if she were a bone he had dragged into his tiger's lair.

No!

Lorne leaped to her feet and ran to the door through which Razul Bey had departed, his great cloak flung over his shoulder, the smoke of his cheroot left in his wake.

She wrenched at the iron handle of the door and pulled it open. The doorway's heavy oval framed a pair of men in robes, their dark eyes inscrutable, their brown faces expressing no emotion in the face of her distress.

Fury rushed over Lorne that she should be treated in this way. A fury laced with fear as she confronted the guards. In the old days the guardians of a *harim* had been eunuchs, but these men, with their heads swathed in snowy turbans that emphasized their hawklike faces, were about as much like eunuchs as Razul Bey himself. Instinctively she knew that they were top security guards in the household of the bey. Men who didn't question what he did, especially when it came to his attitude toward a woman.

One of them reached forward and, with his eyes fixed inscrutably upon Lorne, closed the door in her face with a slow deliberation. Lorne stood there feeling shocked and angry, almost jumping out of her skin when the bead curtain rattled behind her. She swung round, her eyes filled with her distress, and gazed in bewilderment at the young woman who had entered the room.

They stared at each other, as if both of them felt startled by the contrast in their coloring and clothing. The Egyptian girl was darkly beautiful, her almond-shaped eyes outlined with kohl beneath the fine crescents of her eyebrows. Her hair was shiny as jet, her many silk-fine plaits interwoven. Golden hoops glinted in her earlobes, and her carriage was graceful in a honey-colored robe with wide sleeves edged with embroidery.

"I am the Princess Jamaila." She spoke in fluent French, and as she came closer to Lorne, a spicy perfume wafted from her robe, and the golden hoops swung against her dusky-gold cheeks. A provocative tinkle came from the anklets she wore, directing Lorne's glance to slim feet painted with henna in lacy patterns.

Lorne decided that anyone as seductive as this girl, with the title of *princess*, had to be the favorite among the bey's women. From head to heel she looked as if she spent her days and nights in a *harim*, a kind of doll, made to loll among cushions, her only function to be fondled by lean fingers and admired by dark-lashed amber eyes.

A feeling of heat swept Lorne. Her emotions were a mixture of temper and mortification at finding herself in a place such as this. A place where the bey of Karah indulged his masculine desires and was master of all he surveyed.

"I—I must get out of here—" Lorne spoke distractedly in French. "It would surely be to your benefit—to help me?"

The exotic girl eyed Lorne up and down in a deliberate and ironic way. "You think I would invite the anger of the

Lord Razul by doing as you ask?" She smiled at subtle
thoughts. "It is typical of a *roumia* to believe that she has
only to ask in order to receive."

"Surely *you* can't want me here?" Lorne could feel her
heart sinking even as she made the effort to stir the other girl
to jealousy.

"I don't want you here," the princess agreed, "but the
Lord Razul appears to—want you. It would be foolish of me
to assist you in any way that goes against his wishes. Come,
you must wish to refresh yourself with a bath and a change
of attire. The bathing attendants speak only Arabic, so I
shall interpret for you."

The bead curtain was brushed aside, and Lorne followed
reluctantly in the wake of the hennaed feet. They entered the
inner recesses of the *serai*, and Lorne glanced around in a
bemused way, seeing a large room that was utterly Eastern.

A fine mesh of carved, silvery wood screened the long,
deep-silled windows. Tinted lamps shed their light over the
ivory and pearl inlays of the furniture, which stood upon
splendid carpets. Incense twigs burned in a copper brazier,
sending up spirals of scented smoke, and there were velvet
hangings embroidered with fabulous birds and beasts.

Even as Lorne breathed the sensuous scent of the place,
her gaze fell on a wide couch draped in a pavilion of fine
silk, its coverlet reaching, in a shimmer of silk, to the floor.
As she took in the bed, Lorne felt on the verge of going out
of her mind. Her mind seethed with images in which Razul
Kebîr dominated her—there on that bed.

Oh God, her life had gone so desperately astray, and in
desperation she flung round on the Princess Jamaila.

"Haven't you any feelings?" she demanded. "Is everyone in this place as heartless as that—that devil?"

"Perhaps you are the one without a heart," the princess
mocked. "Perhaps you lack the requisite feelings of a
woman."

"I'm most certainly not *his* kind of a woman," Lorne said, turning away from the sumptuous bed with a shudder of distaste. Silk and satin and heaps of cushions—it was a scene all set for a torrid seduction.

In turning from the bed, her gaze fell upon a tapestry, which completely covered one of the walls. In boldly sewn silks, a girl was depicted, her fair hair to her waist as she stood on the verge of withdrawing her hand from a basket of fruit. Some of the fruits were scattered at her bare feet, and the expression on her face was acutely stricken. Her eyes seemed to blaze like the diadem hung around her forehead.

"She was named Rozmonde." A slim, hennaed hand pointed out to Lorne the Arabic script along the border of the tapestry. "She was a crusader's daughter who fell into the hands of a man who kept her in a locked tower, away from his other women. But one of them bribed a eunuch with a jewel, and when Rozmonde's fruit was delivered to her, a scorpion was concealed in the basket. When she reached inside for a peach, or a plum, or maybe a Jaffa orange, she was stung on the hand by the scorpion, and she died."

As she listened, a shiver ran all the way down Lorne's spine, and the silken barbarity of this place and these people was imposed upon her like a palpable touch. Lion had once told her that there were cities in the desert where the residents lived as if time had stopped in its tracks. She had listened to him with fascination, even though the reality of a city among the dunes had been hard to believe in.

Seated there in Lion's study, listening while he talked of his years in the region, the dangers and enticements of the desert had been but part of a story. Now, as she glanced around her, she saw that everything was a vivid reality, like the confusion of Oriental imagery in the woodwork of the windows, so designed that the sun could pierce through and carry the patterns to the floor. So that a woman could look

through the delicate carving but not be seen from the outside.

"I have my pride," she told herself fiercely. Whatever else
was taken from her, no one could take that.

It gave her a dash of courage as she followed the Princess
Jamaila into the bathroom—a misnomer, because the
sunken, lotus-shaped bath would have held a dining table
with a dozen people seated around it. The tiling of the walls
was in raised designs, bold and detailed, in the most gor-
geous turquoise and jade intermingling of colors.

In an alcove stood a massage couch, and there were two
women in robes waiting to attend upon her.

"Please tell them to go away," she said to the princess. "I
can manage perfectly well on my own."

"It is the custom—"

"I don't care a rap what your customs are." Lorne raised
her voice. "They aren't mine, and I won't have an audience
while I take a bath."

"You are that modest?" The princess glanced at the two
women and said something in Arabic. They immediately
smiled, and Lorne guessed the content of the remark.
Whatever her modesty, it wouldn't matter to the master of
the *serai*. His desires were paramount, those of a woman a
mere irritation to be brushed aside.

"I don't doubt that there's little modesty in a place such
as this," Lorne retorted. "I've only to take one look to see
that it's devoted to Razul Bey's demands and pleasures. I'm
not staying here—I have to get out of this place!"

Lorne made a dash for the doorway, hoping wildly that
her display of temperament would gain her the freedom that
was all she desired in the world. The bey was obviously used
to compliance in his women, and her refusal to be com-
pliant could only annoy him.

"Let go!" She thrust the bath attendants out of her way
and ran into the bedchamber. The pair came rushing after
her, and there was a furious tussle, causing Lorne's shirt to

be ripped all the way down the front. Her temper and despair were so aroused that she fought like a she-cat to get free of the hands that clutched at her and tried to subdue her.

In the middle of this affray the bead curtain was thrust aside to admit the cause of Lorne's distraught behavior. "T-tell these wretched women—" she stood there panting, one hand clutching at the torn halves of her shirt "—tell them to leave me alone!"

He rapped something in Arabic, and they hastily retreated into the bathroom, from which the Princess Jamaila emerged. She spoke to him in French, so Lorne would understand.

"Release the *roumia* from your house, cousin. She is more of a nuisance than she's worth—just look at her! Hair like that of a wild woman and a body pale as goat's cheese."

Lorne glowered through the hair that flopped over her forehead, then felt a sudden jolting of her nerves as Razul Bey swept his eyes over her. Tiger eyes that missed not a detail of her disarray, causing Lorne to flush to the roots of her disordered hair. She had been raised from a child to be neat and orderly, both in her behavior and her dress, and this monstrous man had reduced her to a screeching cat whose claws were straining to get at his face.

"Throw me out," she challenged him. "You've had the satisfaction of seeing my grandfather dead, so what is there to be gained from keeping me here? I'm neither beautiful like your princess, nor am I submissive. I'm filled with hate—can't you see that I am?"

"I feel sure," he said smoothly, "that after you have bathed and attired yourself in a garment that is neither torn nor grubby, you will feel a different person. You will relax and take the rest that you need."

"What I need is to be someplace where I never set eyes on your face again." Lorne jerked the hair out of her eyes, which were burning so blue in her face, they were startling.

"Send me to Bar-Soudi and I—I shan't say a word about any of this—" She broke off, hesitated, then added, "I swear I won't."

For tense moments on end he regarded her, then the Princess Jamaila spoke. "Do it, cousin. Be rid of her. She is like a wasp in a window, buzzing with temper and ready at any moment to sting you. Surely you have no need of *her*?"

"Jamaila—" he slowly turned his gaze upon the beautiful, honey-skinned face with its scornful lips "—it isn't yet time for any member of the tribe to give orders to me. You are your father's daughter in every respect, but I am the head of the house, the tents and every inch of the tribal terrain. I do what it suits me to do, without asking permission of any woman, even one as lovely as yourself."

"I have only your welfare at heart, Razul." The almond-shaped eyes flashed a look at Lorne. "I have the feeling that this blue-eyed *roumia* will bring bad luck. Surely it's enough that the old Frenchman is dead? Why bother with the granddaughter?"

"Why, indeed?" The look he was giving Lorne was enigmatic; there was no telling which way he would decide, and she held her breath, praying he would let it rest that she had called him a dog and a liar. Her lips moved.... If it would get her out of this place, then she'd apologize to him.

Strange, almost fateful seconds held them locked in a silence she was about to break, when he swooped, as he had done at L'Oasis and caught her up in his arms. She was too surprised to resist as he strode with her into the bathroom and dropped her into the water-filled bath, which was charging the air with its herbal essences.

Lorne gasped for breath as she plunged about in the sunken bath, while he stood at the rim and laughed down at her.

"Y-you monster!" she spluttered. "You insufferable b-brute—"

"Enjoy your bath," he mocked. "It will calm you down and relax your nerves after your ordeal of last night. You will be grateful for the comforts of the *serai*—after a while."

Lorne's bubble of hope had burst and overwhelmed her, and as the tears filled her eyes she swiveled away from his scrutiny and plunged her head beneath the water. He'd never see her cry—never!

She knew he had gone when the bath attendants started to speak to each other, and with a shrug she tugged off her torn shirt and removed the rest of her clothes. She flung the soggy ball out of her way, then proceeded to wash herself in what, after all, was the most luxurious bath she had ever seen. It was like a lotus made of alabaster, and she could actually swim about in it.

What on earth would the good Sisters say if they could see her right now? They'd be shocked and pitying, she decided, that one of their pupils had landed herself in a place such as this. They'd say Hail Mary's for the preservance of her soul, in the house of an infidel such as Razul Kebîr.

Even in the midst of her self-pity, Lorne had no sweet recollection of childhood, spent as it had been in the chilly, repressive environs of a strictly run school. Coming to live with Lion had seemed like an escape from prison. Seeing the desert for the first time, she had marveled at its magnitude, its glorious solitude that somehow released the spirit, its unbounded freedom after a restrictive way of life.

Each evening the sun was like a fireball in the western sky, then night came quickly, bringing a rush of stars into the velvety sky, and a delicious coolness.

She had quickly learned to ride, and had lost no time becoming the kind of granddaughter Lion had seemed to want. She hadn't dawdled over her lessons as she had in the classroom, rapidly felt at home in the saddle on her Arabian horse, hitting the targets that her grandfather set up for her when he taught her to use a gun.... Why had she hesitated, back there at L'Oasis? She could easily have disabled Razul Kebîr.

And, a small voice whispered in her head, left herself at the mercy of his men, waiting outside in the murk of the dust storm, crouched like figures of doom beside their camels.

They would have been merciless, she knew that. Just like the bey in deliberately shaking her trust in Lion's love for her.

She splashed water as she climbed out of the bath, and immediately one of the attendants was ready with a toweling robe. For the time being a kind of numb acceptance had taken hold of Lorne, and almost like a dummy, she allowed the two women to fuss around her. They dried her hair, then brushed and combed out the tangles. They manicured her toenails and fingernails, and would have painted her with henna had she allowed it. She fiercely shook her head. She knew that Eastern people referred to henna as the flower of joy, and she felt far from joyful.

Biting down on her lip, which held a treacherous tremor, Lorne submitted to being clad in a robe of such delicate silk that she barely felt its presence. She was led into the other room, now vacated by the princess and the bey, and escorted to the couch, which had filled her mind with such shocking images. Now its sumptuous softness, and her own weariness, drew her downward. She slid among the cushions and felt like a trapped moth as the pavilion of silk was closed around her.

As she lay there, Lorne breathed the delicate, perfumed oil in the lamps, whose tinted colors were discernible through the transparent bed drapes. Now she wanted to sleep. Perhaps she might awaken to find that L'Oasis was undamaged by storm and fire. She might hear Lion's voice, vigorously demanding his coffee. She might only have dreamed that a ruthless stranger had carried her off to his palace in the desert.

Curled on her side, holding a cushion as if for comfort,
Lorne drifted off to sleep. She was so worn out by everything that she barely moved in her sleep, her slim body and
limbs showing through the diaphanous fabric of the corn-
colored robe. The satin throw-over on which she lay was a
tawny contrast to her blond hair, which had recovered its
deep wave above her brow, the soft curves of the wave im-
parting to her face a touching vulnerability.

The tall figure opened the bed drapes with a hand that
looked sunburned against the sheer white silk. He gazed intently at Lorne's unaware figure on the bed, his eyes traveling from her blond hair to her slender neck, from her fine-
boned shoulders to her breasts, their tips softly outlined by
the corn-gold silk, which revealed far more than it concealed.

His amber eyes were oblique and shaded heavily by his
dark lashes as he watched at the bedside for moments on
end. His face was a golden mask that gave no indication of
his thoughts or feelings, and at last, as silently as he had
entered, he departed. For the first time in an hour Lorne
stirred, but she didn't wake up. It was as if her body had
sensed the appraisal of the bey's eyes, and in her sleep Lorne
drew back the cushion, which her hands had released, and
pressed it to her like a shield.

She awoke a long time later, so bemused at first that she
believed herself back at L'Oasis. She thought the woman at
her bedside was one of Lion's servants and then realized,
with a catch of her breath that the woman was exception-
ally dark skinned and wearing a multicolored scarf, which
was tied like a turban.

"The *lel-lah* is awake, eh?" The woman leaned toward
Lorne and studied her with bright, curious eyes.

Lorne pulled herself into a sitting position, every detail of
the day rushing back into her mind. Her grandfather and his
house among the fruit groves had been engulfed in flames,
and she was a prisoner in the palace of Razul Kebîr.

"I am Kasha, who was nurse to the Lord Razul when he was a boy." The woman spoke a guttural French, which Lorne had no difficulty in understanding. "His Eminence has asked me to be in your service, *lel-lah*, and I shall do my utmost to please him."

Lorne's lips twisted wryly at the way the words were phrased, and she replied offhandedly, "I don't imagine I shall be staying here for very long, so he needn't have bothered himself. I'm perfectly capable of taking care of myself."

Kasha showed brilliant teeth in a smile that came and went. "How long you stay will be decided by the Lord Razul, and it is customary for a *kadin* to have a body servant."

"That word, what does it mean?" Lorne asked quickly. *"Kadin?"*

"In your country you would say—mistress." As she spoke, Kasha fingered the big silver brooch that pinned her robe at her shoulder. At the same time her dark eyes, almost with gravity, took in the way Lorne shrank against the big cushions of the bed.

"I-I'm nothing of the sort!" Lorne exclaimed. "How dare he say so!"

"It is assumed, *lel-lah*. Why else would he bring you to his *serai*?"

"Because he's a brute a-and a devil! Because he—oh God, I hate him so much!" Lorne shivered with an intensity of emotion that was even more violent than when she had stood at Lion's bedside and, at last, had covered his dead face. The reality of his death had been hard for her to accept, leaving her, as it did, a partial stranger in a strange land.

And this assumption that she was the bey's new mistress—only a polite term for a toy, or a slave—was insufferable. It made her feel and imagine things that were more terrible than the peace and finality of death.

"Perhaps he makes you a little afraid of him." Kasha shrugged as she spoke, too long in the service of a bey to be overly moved by a young girl's reluctance, her fear of the unknown in the shape of a man.

"He makes me wish I'd shot him through the heart!" Lorne looked around the bedroom with hunted eyes at a felicity of furnishing that was a cage and a trap. "I-I didn't dream he would do this. Bring me here and shut me up—like some object from a slave block! He can't do this to me!"

"Shush." Kasha laid a brown hand on Lorne's trembling shoulder. "You will make yourself feverish if you carry on in this way. Had you harmed the bey, then you would have paid the price with more than your body. His men would have cut your throat."

"I'd have preferred that—"

"Non." Kasha shook a wise head. "You are young, with all your life before you."

"What a life!" Lorne exclaimed. "Shut up in this—this bordello!"

Kasha frowned. "It will be for the best if you accept the state of things. The Lord Razul is taken by your blond hair and your white body—the fact that you still have your virginity."

Lorne caught her breath sharply. "How can he possibly be sure of that?"

"Men of the East are rarely fooled in such matters."

"I'm not of the East, I'm from England, and I—I could have had dozens of men."

Kasha smiled broadly. "You would look shopworn if that were the case, *lel-lah*, but instead you tremble with the fears of a girl who has never been with any man. That Razul Bey will be your first man is not something dreadful. He is paramount chief of a great house. He's admired for his courage and his force of character."

"I bet he isn't—loved." Lorne barbed the words with every bit of venom she could muster.

"To love a man of great power takes character in a woman." Kasha flicked her eyes over Lorne, almost as if she saw her as no more than a feather in the bey's bed.

"How many women does he own?" Lorne tossed her hair with contempt.

"Over the years a number of women have been presented to him," Kasha replied.

"So his *serai* is filled to overflowing."

"Does it upset the *lel-lah* to think so?" Kasha poured lemonade from a crystal jug with a silver spout and handed the silver-rimmed glass to Lorne. The lemonade was refreshing, and Lorne drank thirstily.

"I don't care a rap how many women he has. What I don't like is being one of them. Yes, please, I will have some more lemonade."

Kasha replaced the jug and watched Lorne as she sipped her second glass of the cool, lemon-flavored drink that was just on the edge of sweetness. "There are aspects to being a desert lord's woman that have their pleasant side."

"For instance?" Lorne challenged.

"You might make him love you."

Lorne stared in astonishment at Kasha. "I want him to hate me," she retorted. "That way I shall get free of him. I shall behave so tiresomely, so indifferently, that he'll find me a nuisance and a bore, and he'll let me go."

"Will you, I wonder, find him such a bore?"

"We have nothing in common," Lorne argued. "We're from different cultures, different backgrounds. What could we find to—discuss?"

"Perhaps discussions with you, *lel-lah*, are not on his mind."

The meaning in the words jabbed into Lorne like thorns, and the lemonade glass tilted in her nervous hand. She set it aside carefully, gaining time, begging herself not to crumple into a heap of terror at the thought of what Razul Bey had in mind.

"I-I'm not a virgin," she said, finally. "You must go and tell him, Kasha. Tell Razul Bey about my English lover—the soldier I used to meet in secret, w-when I was seventeen. I used to climb over the convent wall, and he'd be waiting for me under an oak tree. I—I couldn't resist him. He was attractive in his uniform, and I let him kiss me—I let him make love to me."

It was a pack of lies, of course, but Lorne felt desperate. If Razul Kebîr could be made to believe that she was soiled goods, then he might not want to touch her. He was proud, hard, ruthless, but the way he had dropped her into the lotus bath suggested a fastidious man where women were concerned.

Lorne kneeled up on the bed, trying not to care that her figure was apparent through the diaphanous robe. She had to behave as if she were immodest. She had to convince Kasha that her story was true.

"It's better for him to know beforehand," she said. "It's because I'm blond and fair-skinned that I look young and innocent, but I'm not. I-I've been kissed all over by my English soldier. I've had his hands all over me, and I've known everything with him, in the wheat field where we used to make love."

Kasha stared hard at Lorne, who caught a flicker of uncertainty in the dark eyes. "I want him to know the truth about me." She spoke with the impetuosity of apparent truth. "If you won't tell him about my soldier, then I shall. He shouldn't be too surprised. He hated my grandfather and implied that he wasn't a man of integrity—he can hardly expect me to be an angel, just because I have blond hair."

Lorne lifted an arm and ran her fingers through her hair, aware that the lamplight made it glisten. She slid from the bed and stood there in the transparent robe, banking down inside her the self-hurt of behaving in this shameless fashion. Two years with Lion Desirée had not eliminated what the nuns had drummed into her and the other pupils, that the flesh was subordinate to the spirit. That the body was selfish, and its appetites only justified if they fed on love.

"Tell him," Kasha said, "but don't be too surprised if he does not send you to Bar-Soudi. Over the years, as I told you, he has been presented with women, but more often than not he has arranged their marriages to officers of his guard. How can you be sure that he won't do the same with you?"

"He wouldn't dare!" Lorne's body went rigid inside the supple silk robe, almost as if touched by fire. "He couldn't be that despicable—could he?"

Kasha shrugged. "There are houses of ill repute, where not all the women have dark skins. My advice, *lel-lah*, is that you be wise and not foolish in dealing with my Lord Razul. Act the angel, if you don't want him to be a devil."

The words bounced about in Lorne's desperate mind.... It was too apparent that she was dealing with a man who had stolen her as casually as a thief who slid his hand into a pocket and removed a wallet. And like the thief, he would take from her what he wanted, then toss her aside.

Lorne gave a characteristic toss of her head, the deep wave bouncing on her brow. "You know him well, don't you, Kasha? You must do, if you looked after him when he was young."

"I know him well enough," Kasha agreed. "Treat him as you would the desert itself. It is in the nature of a man of El Karah to be unpredictable in his dealings with a woman, but if you are clever, then you might make a fortune out of your liaison with him."

Lorne widened her eyes at Kasha, who slowly nodded her head. "He's a generous man, and if you have jewelry, you might be able to buy your freedom."

The very word made Lorne ache with longing to be her own person again, free to dress as she pleased and free to go home to England, where the temperate sun and the cool green countryside didn't make men in the likeness of Razul Kebîr.

He was imprinted on her mind, his stature and his pagan face set with eyes that had held her captive in their amber. Even to see him in her imagination was to feel threatened by his strange personality.

Her thoughts spun her backward to L'Oasis. From his first entrance into the plantation house, she had instinctively known that he meant trouble for her, standing there at the foot of the stairs, wrapped from head to heel in his great cloak. "Your grandfather offered you to me in exchange for L'Oasis," he had said. Lorne could only wonder if he had accepted the offer....

CHAPTER FOUR

WAS IT THERE IN HER LOOKS, there in her eyes that her life would be so disruptive? Lorne stared into the mirror, whose damascened frame seemed to lend a peculiar depth to her reflection, making Lorne feel a stranger to herself in the foreign clothes she was obliged to wear.

The trousers were of hand-loomed pure silk, so delicate to the touch that she felt naked in them. They were clasped to her legs by beaded bands, and above them she was clad in a lovely tunic of pearl and silver, the front of the sleeves being open and linked by strands of pearls.

She had pleaded with Kasha to find her a more simple outfit but had been told that she must look her best when she dined with the Lord Razul. She must bear in mind that when he gave an order, he expected it to be carried out, and he had instructed Kasha that he wanted the English girl to look pleasing.

Her blond hair was left unbound but threaded with fine gold chains that gave her a glittering look. A dusting of kohl had been applied to her eyes, but she had stubbornly refused to wear the other exotic beautifiers contained in a box of black crocodile.

The application of kohl had deepened the blue luster of her eyes, producing a sensuous look that she didn't wish to see in herself. Her gaze seemed mysterious and seductive. Gone, all gone was Lion's tomboy, and she felt sure she looked like a slave girl, brought in by caravan.

Hating the gleam of her legs through the organza trousers, hating every aspect of herself in this environment,
Lorne turned away from the mirror and stood without
expression as Kasha tried to interest her in an array of slim,
glass-stoppered phials, each one holding a perfume and inscribed with Arabian script.

She must choose, Kasha persisted. Each one of the scents
was *atara*, spicy, and would make her smell fragrant. Lorne
turned up her nose and selected one of the phials at random. She drew out the stopper and was assailed by a scent
that seemed as if it wafted in from a jasmine garden. Even
as the image entered her head, she wanted to dispel it. Such
romantic images had no place in her mind. Not for an instant must she allow this place to beguile her; she must stay
indifferent to everything—scents and colors and the silken
barbarity of it all.

"This one will do," she said and tipped some of it onto
her bare wrists. She smiled ironically as she did so. Scent had
been banned at the convent school, and when she had come
to live at L'Oasis, she had worn shirts and breeches in the
daytime and in the evenings had dressed in simple frocks
without any touch of glamour. Even visits to the *souk* in
Bar-Soudi had not tempted her to buy the Eastern per-
fumes that were distilled on the premises of a tiny shop, dim
with shadows and spicy with scent.

"Do you approve, Kasha?" She held out a wrist to the
woman who might become her one and only friend in the
palace. She could have no secrets from Kasha, whose
friendship she needed, if she was to keep her sanity, locked
up in this outlandish place whose very location was a mystery to her.

Kasha took the scent phial from Lorne and firmly replaced the stopper. "On the skin it is harmless," she said,
"but a few drops taken internally would kill you."

"Attar of poison." Lorne smiled. "How appropriate for
a dinner date with his barbaric lordship. Perhaps I should

take the phial of scent with me—mmm, that's an interesting idea, isn't it?"

"An idea you had better forget." Kasha put away the scents, each one allocated to a fascinating little drawer, either painted with a flower or a bird. Lorne noticed that the fragrant poison was put into a drawer with a black plumed bird on it, and with a look in her eyes that made her resemble Lionel Desirée, she raised a wrist and sniffed her skin. The pearls glimmered along her arms, looking like jeweled shackles.

Kasha looked her over critically as she stood there, upward from her silver slippered feet to her gold-stranded hair. "The Lord Razul will be pleased with you," she said, a slight note of uncertainty in her voice. There was a delicately damascened look about Lorne in the Eastern clothes. She looked strange in them, like a fragile carving of gold and silver.

Lorne smiled wryly. "I look odd, don't I?" Clothes like these were meant to be worn by a voluptuous brunette, and Lorne knew that she was almost as slim as a boy, and that she actually looked at her best in riding wear. "All to the best, Kasha. I don't want to look too fanciful."

"You are—different," Kasha said slowly, with a note of meaning in her voice that sent a shiver through Lorne. She had an unusual innocence, created by her years at the convent, and by her isolation at L'Oasis, but her instincts were coming painfully alive in the *serai*. This was the house of Razul Bey's women, and she hadn't been brought here on a visit. She couldn't pretend to herself that she would be treated like a guest. Razul Kebîr had already kissed her with a devastating unconcern for her feelings.

That she had the sensibility of her youth. That she had been hurt and grieved by the loss of Lion seemed of little matter to him.

Gritting her teeth, Lorne turned again to the damascened mirror. She gazed at herself as if she were halluci-

nating. That pearl and silver creature in the looking glass
was as unreal as an idol, and even as she felt a frantic urge
to tear the garments from her body, a tall, imposing figure
came silently into the room and took a stance that reflected
him behind her.

He regarded her in silence, and she couldn't tell from his
face what he thought of her appearance. Eyes burning, she
swung to face him, but it was a mistake. Instantly she became aware of his proximity... his stature and air of dominance in a kaftan of heavy, somber silk, jewel-clasped at the
throat. Dark, tapering trousers hugged the muscles of his
legs, and his feet were thrust into saffron-colored slippers.

He looked every inch the powerful desert lord, who, in
Lorne's emotional state, was handsome and terrible as some
ruler of the cruel old days, who had necks broken at the
slightest sign of rebellion.

"Well, *habibti*, you look so much better for a bath and a
sleep." His eyes slid over her, taking in every detail of her
appearance. He turned and said something in Arabic to
Kasha, who quickly left them on their own.

"These clothes—" The words broke from Lorne. "I look
absurd in them. I feel like an odalisque."

"You look rather like one." His lips expressed amusement. "But just think, I could have suggested that you dine
with me in a chemise, such as the one you slept in."

Lorne stared up at him, taking in the black sideburns that
thrust with a daggerlike precision against his jaws. He
looked vigorously alive and in command, showing not a care
for anyone's destiny except his own.

"Femme blonde," he murmured, "you have eyes that
shimmer like jewels. What are you thinking, eh?"

"I thought you had access into everyone's thoughts," she
rejoined. "I suppose you sneaked in here while I was asleep
a-and took a good look at me?"

"I took a look at you," he confessed, "but whether or
not my intentions were good..."

"They wouldn't be," she accused. "Y-you have no right to—to treat me like one of those women, those given to you as if they're no more than boxes of candy. I'm English—"

"You are partly French, which is why you have a certain fire in you. The blond hair and the Gallic temperament are an intriguing combination. Fire and frost."

"You are overbearing, unscrupulous and arrogant," she shot back at him.

"Is that all?" he drawled. "Surely there is more, and it's best that you get it off your chest before we partake of dinner. I wouldn't want you to have indigestion."

"You're an insufferable bully," she flung at him. "Just because you have a title, you're ingrained with the idea that you are superior to me and can do as you please. It's criminal, what you're doing to me!"

"What am I doing?" he mocked. "It seems to me that you have luxurious quarters, and you are wearing a garment that must have cost a lot of money."

"Don't you keep an account of what you spend on clothes for your—concubines?" Lorne asked scornfully.

"There's little necessity," he rejoined.

"And what is that supposed to mean, Lord Razul?"

"Surely your vivid imagination can supply the details." His eyes were brutally mocking. "The *serai* of a bey is neither Ascot nor Paris. During the day the weather here in El Karah is very warm. In such circumstances a woman would feel most at ease in the least possible clothes, for as you are aware the Eastern woman spends the greater part of the day inside the house. It's in the cool of the evening that she goes to the roof garden or terrace, and that is where you and I are going to enjoy dinner."

He reached out and took Lorne firmly by the hand. "Come, the cool air of the roof garden will help you to simmer down. By Allah, if I didn't know you were Lionel Desirée's granddaughter, I would guess it."

Lorne went with him in a mutinous frame of mind. They crossed a courtyard hung with starlight and the scent of flowers trailing over old stone walls. They entered a fretted tower through an archway, where a narrow flight of steps led in a steep spiral to the roof of the palace.

Lanterns were set in wall niches to offset the pitchy darkness of the stairway, and in Lorne's turbulent mind the place and the man blended into a strange kind of dream, where she walked like a dreamer.

They stepped out upon a battlemented roof, above which the stars were brilliant and clustering in a sky like velvet. A pair of discreet, white-clad servants were already there to wait upon them at a silver-chased table set upon a magnificent rug that was spread on the ground, thick and soft as fleece, and scattered with floor cushions, banks of them in softest leather.

Lorne stood, amazed by it all, her face bemused in the tinted light from the lanterns, peacock green, topaz and ruby.

"Be seated."

She cast a look at the man who had ordered this romantic-looking dinner. Behind those heavy-lashed eyes he was an uncaring, ruthless brute, yet in his kaftan of somber royal blue, gemmed at his bronzed throat by an equally somber jewel, he looked proud and distinguished. A barbarian with a veneer of culture, Lorne told herself. A Janus with two faces, like golden masks that he could exchange as the mood took him.

"The food will get cold." He gestured at the rug, and Lorne slid down among the cushions. He did the same, and she was indescribably aware of him beside her, her nostrils tensing to the aroma of his skin, her eyes fixed upon his brown hands as they unfolded a linen serviette.

"Are you hungry?" he asked.

As she hesitated, determined to be indifferent to his Janus-faced charm, slices of watermelon and giant shrimps

were served, and they looked too appetizing to be resisted.
Her eyes widened as a pale golden wine was poured into a
pair of crystal glasses. It was a wine distilled from dates,
Razul Bey told her, as he broke a shrimp apart and ate it.
"Taste it, *habibti*."

She did so, wondering what meaning was contained in the
name he gave her.

"Is the wine to your liking?" He quizzed her face, and the
lantern light was mirrored in his eyes. They held her like the
lambent yet dangerous gaze of a tiger.... He most closely
resembled the big cat with its terrible beauty when he concealed his menace and pretended to be civilized.

"It is rather nice," she had to admit. "Is it intoxicat-
ing?"

"Perhaps, to a palate like yours."

She ate watermelon and a delicious chunk of shrimp and
gave him an enquiring look. At the dinner table it was almost impossible to be as distant and tiresomely boring as she
had planned to be. The food was too exceptional...the
company too provocative.

"You have never indulged your appetites," he said,
drinking from his own glass. "The whites of your eyes are
like crystal. As a matter of fact, your eyes are a lovely, very
unusual color. They intensify your fairness of skin and
hair."

"I don't want your flattery, Lord Razul." She put frost-
ing on her voice, and the look she gave him was murder-
ous. "I'm no beauty—I merely look different from all your
other women."

"All my other women," he mocked, leaning an elbow on
one of the big cushions, big and supple and totally at his
ease. "Just how many have you in mind?"

"I—I expect there are quite a few." She drank some more
wine and evaded the disturbing deeps of his eyes. Their
amber held the lantern light, as did the striking planes of his

face. His blue, beautifully wrapped turban added to his strangeness.

"Does it concern you?" He tilted an eyebrow. "Would you like to be the only piece of sugar in my cup?"

"I'd like to be the drop of poison," she said emphatically.

His reaction was to laugh, a sound that seemed to erupt from deep in his chest. "You are never lost for a rejoinder, are you? But your wit, *habibti*, is a pleasure rather than a pain."

"I thought men of El Karah liked women to be subdued, with few opinions of their own?" Through the veil of her lashes she watched him as their first-course plates were removed and replaced by a large dish under an elaborate silver dome.

A smile curled on his mouth, which was as ruthlessly detailed as all his features. "Have you ever eaten *couscous*?" he asked, as if biding his time before replying to her question.

She shook her head, her nostrils tensing as the servant lifted the dome of the big dish and revealed a mound of smoking semolina, implanted with chunks of meat and chicken, and surrounded by tiny marrows in gravy, sweet corn and potatoes, and baby carrots. Not only did the dish of food look inviting, it smelled heavenly, and Lorne felt her mouth watering.

"It is traditional to eat from the one dish, but you may use a fork and a spoon—unless, of course, you prefer to use your fingers?"

"Oh—no." Lorne was too rigidly trained by the nuns in England to be able to pick up a chicken leg, as he did, and casually bite off the meat with his strong teeth. She was aware that he watched with amusement as she plunged into the semolina with fork and spoon, quite unable to imitate his dexterity in rolling the semolina into balls, which he tossed into his mouth.

Lorne felt certain that he had deliberately chosen this intimate style of eating, as if to underline his foreign ways, as if to let her know that she had to learn how to live with his habits.

"How astonishing that the grandchild of Lionel Desirée should have reservations of any sort." He ate not only with a total lack of reservation, but it rather annoyed her to see that nothing spilled from his fingers. He made her feel clumsy by comparison, for she had to use her fork to eat her meat and vegetables.

"I—I don't want to talk about my grandfather," she said, dabbing gravy from the side of her mouth. "I don't want to listen to your insults about him."

He reacted with a casual shrug. "What would you like to talk about? Shall we talk of the desert? It has many names, you know, and has been called the garden of desire."

"It's a place of blistering heat." She infused scorn into her voice, as if she had felt none of the magic of the desert at dawn or the glory of the sun dying in splendor, painting the sky and the sands with an artistry no man or woman had fully achieved on canvas.

"Then why remain at L'Oasis, surrounded by the desert?"

"I had nowhere else to go—" Lorne broke off, realizing too late that he had trapped her with his question. "It's none of your business what I think or feel."

"You have made no secret of your feelings for me," he drawled.

"It must make a change for you, Lord Razul, to be despised from the bottom of a woman's heart."

"Do you imagine that all other women are besotted with me?"

"I daresay you like to think so, and I expect they're too afraid of you to tell you any different."

"You aren't shaking in your shoes, eh?"

"You're a desert libertine, and I detest you for bringing me here."

"To my house of unbridled lusts, eh?" He laughed as he spoke and gestured for the removal of the main-course dish. "Perhaps pancakes *diable* will sweeten that vitriolic tongue of yours, or would you prefer sliced figs in a jelly of pomegranate juice?"

"I've had enough to eat."

He waved away her objection and spoke in Arabic to the manservant who hovered at the table. He departed to carry out the bey's order, while the other servant presented bowls of orange-flower water, in which they cleansed their hands, drying them on embroidered towels.

Lorne gazed up at the stars and felt as if she trembled in all that infinity, lost in time and poised for a dangerous fall. Her gaze fell to the battlemented wall of the rooftop, and she had a sudden reckless urge to run to the wall and, without pausing, leap through one of those gaps in the stonework to the stony pavement of the courtyard far below.

"Come, *habibti*, admit that you find the desert unique."

With a shiver she came back out of her dark thoughts and looked at the man beside her, who was fondling with his brown fingers the crystal stem of his wineglass. "That mountain range that you can see in the starlight is the Ghelb e Ahib," he said. "But you don't know Arabic, do you? You don't know what the name means?"

Lorne shook her head and barely cared to know. The desert and the mountains were all part of her prison, like the palace itself, its bastions and turrets outlined against the sky, like a silver and sable tapestry.

"That range is known as the Heart of the Slave." With casual enjoyment Razul Bey savored his wine. "One of these days we shall ride there, for the villages that cling to its slopes are part of my terrain."

"One of these days?" she exclaimed. "Just how long are you planning on keeping me here?"

He didn't answer right away, but let his eyes roam over her indignant face. "Let us say, until you no longer amuse me."

"Blast your arrogance—" Lorne's fingers clenched around the finger bowl, and she was preparing to hurl the contents in his face when he reached forward and stayed her hand.

"I wouldn't try it," he murmured. "I might be tempted to drench you in return."

"I—I wouldn't put anything past you." Lorne nursed her wrist, for his grip hadn't been gentle. "From what I hear, you took over from the old *cadi* without batting an eyelid."

"True, I came to power by selection not inheritance." His eyes held her in almost an hypnotic way, flickering gold and green in the sway of the lanterns. "His son lacked what it takes to be a leader, and though the daughter, the Princess Jamaila, has more spirit, the tribe would not have found a woman acceptable."

"Naturally." Lorne curled her lip. "They wouldn't find it belittling to take orders from such as you, would they? You personify all they look up to, especially in your attitude to women. You're a walking example of male superiority, not to mention greed. Now you have L'Oasis—or what's left of it."

"There are wells on the land." The resonance of bronze rang in his voice.

"From your attitude, Lord Razul, I thought there had to be oil wells, at least."

He swept a curt look over her face. "You have the intellect of a schoolgirl. You are less instructed in the ways of life than the youngest *bint* in the province of El Karah. You need tuition in the ways of being a woman."

"And you are going to be my teacher?" She tried to speak the words with a cool indifference, but there was a suggestiveness in his remark that stoked her smoldering, deep-down fear of his intentions. "You'd like to beat me down into a heap at your feet, but you'll never do it!" she asserted, more bravely than she felt.

"You think not?" He leaned closer to her, everything about him so arrantly male. "The aspects of a country formulate the character of a person, but when you came to the desert, your needs underwent a change. For example, you discovered how exciting it is to ride across the tawny sands. Ah, did you imagine that you were never under surveillance when you rode?"

"By you?" she exclaimed.

"Of course. Would I not be curious about the girl from the convent school in England, who was supposed to have all the virtues?" His eyelids drooped in a smile, and a gleam of curiosity lay behind the intent look he was giving her. It was as if he was searching out the girl in the school uniform, her hair tightly braided and kept as restrained as its wheaten vitality would allow. His gaze slid downward and took in her slim legs, revealed through the fine silk trousers that her teachers would have regarded as sinful in the extreme.

Lorne flushed and felt a sweeping relief as the manservant appeared with dessert, along with the implements for *café filtre*, and a selection of fruit, nuts and sweets.

She ate the sliced figs in a delicious jelly with a silent intentness, as if willing time not to move. But when the coffee was poured, the servant cleared away the plates and departed. They were alone on the roof of the palace, beneath a cloak of stars, the air so still that the aromas of the night were trapped like a strange essence, mingling with the tang of coffee and the mixture of fruits in a plaited basket. Black grapes, almost the size of damsons, smooth-skinned nectarines, plump dates and tangerines.

At any other time Lorne would have felt tempted by the luscious-looking fruit, but tension had her in its grip. She was intensely aware that Razul Bey didn't intend anyone to disturb them now that dinner was over.

"Such a night," he murmured. "I would like to smoke a cigar, if you have no objection."

"None at all," she said quickly, only too glad to see his hands occupied with his lighter and cigar, whose smoke added its pungency to the night scents.

He lounged among the cushions, the wide sleeves of his kaftan falling back from his muscular forearms, showing the dark hair against his golden skin. He was a human tiger in Lorne's eyes, without a bone of regret in his body for anything he did. His Eminence, the *padishah*, who could do as he pleased where a woman was concerned.

"Women have no souls in your culture, so they don't really count, do they?" The look of him, so much at his ease, had fanned Lorne's temper back into a flame.

"Allah gave them other attractions, other charms," he said lazily.

"And you think you have a right to those charms, don't you, whether or not the woman is agreeable?"

"It's amazing how agreeable a woman can be made to feel." His hand moved, and Lorne felt something fall glittering and gleaming into her lap.

"What's this?" She gazed down into her lap as if he had thrown a scorpion at her.

"Every woman should have some jewelry. Not so much as a café dancer, but choice pieces that suit her."

"It's a diamond." Still she didn't touch what lay there, smoldering with a fire that was deep in its heart.

"A diamond seems to match your icy fire, would you not agree?"

"I—don't want it!"

"You should never say no to something worth having." Smoke drifted from his lips and formed a veil about his eyes as they watched her reaction to his gift. "It's a very fine stone, hung on a fine chain of genuine gold. Do put it on. I would like to see you wearing it."

"I tell you, I don't want it!" Lorne wanted to throw the big diamond back at him, but something stayed her hand, perhaps the realization that he would force her to wear the pendant, and she would have his hands touching her.

Then, insidiously, there stole into her mind what Kasha had said to her...that if she had jewelry, she might be able to buy her freedom.

Tentatively, as if the stone would come alive and snap at her, Lorne lifted the pendant out of her lap, feeling its weight and watching the way its facets danced with hidden fire. Oh yes, there wasn't a doubt that it was worth a lot of money, and the arrogant donor of it had to feel very sure of his dominance over his people not to care that he gave her a stone of such worth. A diamond that might prove very tempting to someone.

"Put it on," he said again.

Slowly she did so, feeling the tug of the stone against the chain on which it was suspended, there against the skin of her neck, the diamond madly glittering and superbly heart shaped.

"It makes me feel like an exotic dancer," she said tersely.

He looked amused by her remark. "Do you dance, *habibti*?"

"No—and if I did, it wouldn't be to your liking." She had a fleeting but vivid image of herself being forced to dance with a gem in her navel. She had now and again caught glimpses of such dancers in the cafés of Bar-Soudi, coins suspended along their brows, eyes made up with lashings of kohl, hips swaying sinuously to the music of flute and drum.

Such glimpses of Eastern life had been intriguing, but now that Lorne found herself at the very center of a *ménage*, she was tormented by a very different kind of feeling.

"Were you not taught to say thank-you when given a present?"

"I—I don't expect to be given presents. They're only payment, aren't they?"

He slowly raised an eyebrow. "So now I am paying you for your displays of temper and your venomous remarks about my character."

Her fingers clenched the stone. "I can't help it if you're a criminal, can I?"

His eyes narrowed until he was looking at her through rows of lashes. "I am the rapacious villain, and you my fair captive, eh?"

"Yes."

He reacted with a casual shrug of his shoulders, taut and powerful beneath the somber silkiness of his kaftan. "That is how it looks, but has it not occurred to you that I may be asserting my rights?"

"Your—what?" Her pulses gave a turbulent leap. Was it true, then, that Lion had entered into some infamous agreement with him? It was something she dreaded to believe, but there had been that awful look on her grandfather's dying face. He had, on the brink of death, cried out something she had not understood.

"You are dealing with a man of El Karah." He paused a moment, his eyes fixed upon her face. "We believe in retribution, and what is a woman compared to the willful destruction of a large house?"

Lorne slowly relaxed at his reply and breathed more easily. "So I'm here, Lord Razul, because I burned down the plantation house?"

"Of course." He drew his gaze from her face and watched the sky, where a star suddenly blinked and fell out of sight. "A falling star, in our mythology, is an arrow flung by Allah at a demon trying to peer into paradise."

"Which must be overcrowded with men," Lorne said pointedly. "The Koran states, doesn't it, that only men attain heaven when they die?"

"It is to be hoped that a few attain it while they live." He stubbed the end of his cigar and casually reached into the fruit basket for the bunch of black grapes. He broke off a laden stem and handed it to Lorne.

"Thank you," she said, emphatically polite.

"So a few grapes please you more than a diamond, eh?" He studied her as he popped a grape into his mouth and crunched it. "Were you taught by the nuns to regard worldly goods of little value?"

"Yes, as a matter of fact." Her teeth broke into a grape, which was sweet but not cloying, the seeds very small compared to its size. It was perfectly plain that Razul Kebîr didn't regard luxuries as an indulgence that would harm his heavenly chances.

"Hence your lack of hesitation when you set fire to L'Oasis."

"That rankles with you, Lord Razul, doesn't it?" she murmured.

"It occurs to me that you destroyed interior belongings that became yours when Lionel Desirée died."

"What would I do with furniture and family portraits, when you intended to turn me out of the place?" Lorne shivered, then lowered her gaze from his, her head slightly bowed, her hair tumbling forward to veil her face. "I'm not sorry I burned it down. I believe Lion would have wanted that."

"His pagan funeral—minus the dog at his feet."

She flung back her hair with a defiant gesture. "If Lion had pride and defiance, then did you really expect me to be any different?"

"Your pride and defiance are those of an unbroken filly, with a streak of wildness in you."

She pushed at her hair, as she did when distracted. The blue of her eyes was intensified by her emotional state, and a wanton curl clung to the side of her neck. "I—I know what you've got in mind—you rapist!"

The word and all it implied hung in the air between them, then he said softly: "*Diable de femme*, you are asking for a lesson you would not forget in a hurry."

Suddenly he moved, with that same tigerlike agility that had disarmed her at L'Oasis. He had hold of her, among the cushions on the fleecy thickness of the carpet, before she knew where she was. He had her pinned beneath his muscular body, her hands gripped in his so she couldn't claw at his face. He gazed down at her, a menacing look in his eyes.

CHAPTER FIVE

LORNE WRITHED BENEATH HIM, trying with all her might to slither free of his hold on her. He laughed at her futile efforts, showing the white perfection of his teeth, his eyes the brazen gold of the desert as he ran his gaze over her blond hair, in disarray against the cushions.

"Now defy me," he breathed. "Now call me a dog and rapist. Come, I dare you to say those things to my face, in your present position."

"I wish you in hell!" She glared up at him. "You're an egotistical monster. Your high and mighty title doesn't suit your low-down behavior. Oh, how I wish I were a man!"

He laughed at the very idea. "My list of crimes might be a mile long in your estimation, *ma femme*, but I don't go in for unnatural practices."

"Y-you go in for bullying," she shot back at him, the furious contortions of her body frustrated by his hold on her. His closeness was unbearable, and she tried desperately to thrust a knee into his body, but he had her too well trapped for such a maneuver, his legs firmly clasping hers.

It was humiliating to be held in such a position, rampant with intimate possibilities he could so easily have put into practice. Lorne could have wept, except that she had sworn to herself that she wouldn't give him the satisfaction of seeing her in tears. "I bet those who voted you into power are biting their fingers," she said, infusing into her eyes every bit of contempt she could muster.

"I shall bite you, if you don't take care." And with barely any effort he shifted his grip, so her hands were locked above her head in his left hand, exposing her slender neck, which he encircled with his free hand.

"Do your damnedest," she said grandly. "You'd have to use torture before I'd ever *want* you to touch me. I'm just like Lion, you see. I can't stand you!"

"I am heart stricken, *mon amour.*" His lips curled around the words, and his fingers tightened against her throat. Lorne didn't struggle against the pressure, instead she defiantly offered her neck to the lean power of his hand.

He gazed down at her with an unfathomable smile in his eyes, then he began to stroke her neck, gradually sliding his fingers down to the row of pearl buttons that fastened her tunic. Slowly, one by one, he undid the buttons until the diamond on its slender chain lay between her breasts like a huge teardrop. Lorne maintained an icy silence, but it took every ounce of her willpower to act as if she didn't feel his fingers against her body, fondling the diamond and playing its lambent fire over her skin.

"Upon entrance into the *serai* a girl is given a new name." He watched with slumbrous interest the play of colors in the diamond, dancing over her fair skin. "Yours will be Memlik."

"I shan't answer to it," she assured him, every inch of her in the grip of tension as she felt the random touches of his hand. "I expect it has some soulless meaning, or you wouldn't apply it to me."

"It means pale possessed one," he mocked. His eyes roamed over her hair and skin, a look which made her writhe, inside and out. "I think the name is appropriate."

Lorne could no longer bear to look at him ... looking at her. Her lashes swept downward, but she felt him when he leaned over her and imposed upon her the warm, sexual menace that emanated from his firm and forceful body.

"Inshallah," he murmured. "Allah's will is no more to be fought than a sirocco, such as the one that blasted L'Oasis."

"More likely the will of the devil!" Her eyes opened to his face, the skin deeply golden and close-grained over the Eastern bones—oh yes, his was a marvelously detailed face, but Lorne hated to the depths of her being the way he was regarding her. The way he held her, so that he imposed the vigorous strength and potency in every fiber of his body.

Down to his very heels he was ruthless, and she knew it, and her only weapon of defense was to feign indifference to his touch. He wasn't accustomed to that kind of reaction from a woman. He wasn't used to a female who lay in his arms as if enduring the attentions of an uncouth brute.

Lorne lay there like a figure of ice, forcing herself not to jerk her head when he put his lips to her cheek. "I am not going to rape you." His smile was slow and taunting. "Our women are taught from childhood to be pleasing in the company of a man, and I am going to teach you everything that an Eastern girl is taught. Slowly you will learn, and gradually you will respond to every command that I feel like making. Your body will ignore all commands but mine."

She flinched from his words—she wouldn't believe that what he said was possible. She was her own person and would remain so, no matter what he did to her.

She quivered and seemed to go boneless as he trailed his warm lips down the side of her left breast. "Rest assured, Memlik, I have no inhibitions at all, and you will be taught not to have them. But slowly, *ma femme*, piece by piece, until I have only to lay a finger upon you to have you enslaved, like a little wildcat, petted until you purr only for me."

"Cats scratch as well as purr," she flung back at him. Her fingernails flexed in his grip, and he softly laughed.

"You would like to scratch out my eyes, wouldn't you?"

"It's the only pleasure I'd ever feel in relation to you, my lord."

"I could prove that statement a very foolish one." And so saying, he touched his lips to the pulse that beat visibly at the base of her throat. He moved his lips back and forth, teasing her skin with their touch until Lorne began to feel the most disturbing sensations. As his lips traveled along her collarbone, a most unwanted thrill traveled all the way down her body.

She lay stony still, afraid that he would sense what he was doing to her. When his lips found their way to more intimate portions of her body, she had to fight with herself, lie to herself that what he was doing was indecent.

But her flesh and nerves were treacherous allies in her battle against him. His mouth had a marauding warmth; his touch was the tutored one of a man few women had resisted. He knew her body better than she knew it herself, and she felt his eyes wandering her face, watching for her reaction to his caressing hand.

Lorne flushed to see him watching her. *"Monstre sacré!"* The words came in a burst of breathlessness. "Take your hands off me!"

"I couldn't forgo the pleasure," he taunted her. "But naturally you feel a little shy, for I have heard that convent schoolgirls even bathe in a chemise, just in case they catch sight of their own bodies."

"Y-you're a wicked devil of a man!" Lorne tried to writhe away from him, for now he was holding the sparkling diamond in his fingers and caressing her with it. He moved it teasingly over her bare skin.

"Stop doing that—" She spoke through clenched teeth. "Haven't you any respect?"

"You think it disrespectful, that I caress you with a gem?"

"It's—depraved."

He raised an eyebrow in amusement. "Perhaps inventive, which is another matter." And he let his gaze wander slowly down her body, as if he had in mind further inventiveness. "I will prove that you are *très sensuelle*, as most women are in the hands of a patient man."

"A man who has learned the tricks of the trade, I suppose you mean?" Try as she might Lorne couldn't control the sensory tremors that were going on inside her. It was torture, but of a kind she had never imagined. It was the will of her body being set against the will of her mind, and Razul Bey knew exactly how to get under her skin. He had probably done this a thousand times to other women who had fallen into his lean, subtle, knowing hands.

"Damn you! You're heartless—"

"Ah, no." His lips brushed her skin, shiveringly. "If I were so, then I would take you here and now, *ma femme*, while you are helpless in my hands."

Having said this, he then leaned away from her, releasing the diamond so that it fell between the rise and fall of her breasts. He let go of her hands, but she was too strangely dazed to do instantly what she wanted to do, to close the beaded tunic and hide herself from his eyes.

"God—how much I hate you!" Her fingers fumbled with the pearl buttons as a wave of shame swept over her. She had craved an icy poise that would protect her against Razul Bey, and the unrealized sensuality of her own body had shaken her to the depths. She didn't dare to think of what else lay in store for her as she fumbled her way back to a look of respectability.

"Have you not enjoyed our *dîner à deux*?" He was lighting another cigar, with a hand as steady as a rock. This infuriated Lorne, whose limbs still felt so oddly languid.

"The food was fine," she retorted. "It's the company that I find unbearable."

Smoke drifted from his lips as he watched her brushing a hand over her hair in an effort to make it tidy. Kasha had woven the gold chains into it, and she couldn't tug them free without tugging her hair out by the roots. But the very feel of the chains, hair-fine as they were, made her feel like Razul Bey's object, something for him to torment until he grew tired of the game.

"I look at you," he said, "and it amazes me that such a temper is hiding behind your blue eyes. The nuns must have found you something of a problem. I think you were a young rebel who didn't take too readily to their discipline, nor their fish pie and boiled potatoes, eh?"

"What I am, Lord Razul, and what I feel, is none of your business." She sat there with her hands gripped together in her lap, still feeling the passionate beat of her heart and intensely aware that he was master of the situation. His hands didn't shake as he raised his cigar to his lips and drew on it with lazy pleasure. His nerves were quite under control.

"Contrary to what you say, *ma femme*, what you are and what you feel is very much my business."

"You don't own me!" She was determined not to be beaten down. "I'm here completely against my will, and we both know it!"

"You bartered your own freedom, and you know that." His voice was suddenly as hard as bell metal. "You committed a willful act of arson, which I consider ten times worse than my action in bringing you here. I told you! Call me a dog of a liar and you pay me back, and your only source of revenue is yourself. I think I make myself clear?"

"Transparently." Lorne jerked her chin in the air, resolved on a display of courage, even as the look of him and his metallic tone of voice played havoc with her nerves. His air of mastery was as infuriating as it was total, the *padishah* of El Karah, whose standard flew from a mast above the palace.

"You're full of your power over ordinary mortals," she added. "While I draw breath I'll go on despising you."

"I can't recall that I have asked you to love me." He shrugged his shoulders, the lantern colors playing over their width, and caught somberly in the jewel at his strong brown throat. "Love is a delusion. A desert mirage of palm trees and cool water that vanishes into rock and sand when we reach what had promised to be an oasis. The man or woman who believes in the substance of a mirage is a fool who goes into the desert without taking a waterskin."

"You speak in riddles, Lord Razul."

"We are known for it, Memlik."

"I—I'm Lorne, and I don't wish to be tagged with a foreign name."

"Too bad." He studied the stars that clustered above the palace roof, his cigar poised an inch or two from half-smiling lips. He was like some prince of darkness, Lorne told herself. Some devil in silk, whose superb air of assurance made her own insecurity all the harder to bear.

"T-this entire situation is bizarre. You know you can't keep me here—it's against the law." Even yet Lorne harbored the faint hope that she would strike through his armor and find him vulnerable in an unexpected place. Surely he couldn't be so heartless as not to see her point of view? She couldn't help it that he and Lion had been daggers drawn. She was a separate individual, an Englishwoman on her father's side.

"Whose law?" he enquired. "In this region I am paramount chief, and anyone uninvited is a trespasser on my land, and I'm entitled to mete out whatever punishment suits my mood."

"You—you're insufferable!" she blurted.

"So you keep telling me, but I'm being very lenient in the circumstances. You are aware that two years ago your grandfather became a trespasser, under any law of the land."

"Then why didn't you have him evicted? Two years is a long time—" Lorne broke off, for the significance of those two years' grace struck her speechless. That was when she had come to L'Oasis, and it was possible that Lion had used her, possibly her homelessness, in order to retain some hold on the plantation. Quite out of the blue he had sent for her. She had been astounded when Sister Superior had told her to pack her belongings because she was leaving on a flight already booked for her, and her destination was the house of the grandfather who had never sent her a birthday card or shown any interest in her existence—up to that point in time.

"Is the truth infiltrating?" asked Razul Bey.

"If the pair of you came to some arrangement, then why did you wait to collect on the deal?" Lorne felt heartsick, for she was becoming convinced that Lionel Desirée had cared precious little about her.

"Desirée spun me a tale about a sad little schoolgirl, whose mother had died at her birth, whose father had taken a second wife who didn't want to be bothered with the first wife's child. It was all very emotional . . . and then he added that if I fancied to add an Anglo-French girl to my collection of *kadins*, he would be happy to oblige. This girl from England, as he called you, would need to make adjustments to her surroundings. After all, she had spent years in a convent school and it would be necessary to acclimatize her to the desert and its people."

"He didn't . . . he couldn't have said that . . ." Lorne said pleadingly.

But the man who confronted her had a face of bronze. "You know so little of men and their motivations, and it's time for you to grow up and face reality. Desirée had given all his love and care to L'Oasis, and your mother, his only child, had chosen to leave him for an English stranger. The old colonialism was stamped into his very bones, much as the traditions of El Karah are stamped into mine, and he carried in his heart a revengeful feeling toward your parents, which was constantly fed by his years of isolation."

Razul Bey paused, drew smoke from his cigar and then stubbed it out with deliberation. "But this I will tell you, *ma femme*. This conversation I had with him, yourself the topic, took place before you arrived at L'Oasis. It is possible—just possible—that his stony heart was a little melted by you. Who knows? He's dead now and can't confirm or deny a change of heart."

"You came to the plantation one evening—" Lorne took a deep breath, as if to ease the leaden feeling around her heart. "I overheard you in argument with Lion. Had you come to collect what you were offered, Lord Razul?"

"What do you think?" His eyes were intent upon her face, which had a haunted look in the play of jewel-colored light from the lanterns. "Be as candid as you like."

"I—I believe that Lion came to care for me, and when the time came—he wouldn't let you near me."

There was a drawn-out silence, then Razul Bey gave a laugh. "Do you somehow imagine that I became overpowered by a longing for you, fueled by the picture of you riding in the desert? Do you imagine that my ardor was fired by you? That I felt a want for the boyish girl with the blond hair? Is that what you fondly believe?"

Lorne stared back at him, trying to read his face and failing. "I find you as enigmatic as the desert, Lord Razul. I think you a ruthless and arrogant man who could be capable of anything. Lion had his plantation on your land for many years, and I believe you were fueled by feelings of revenge. I may only have lived in the East for a couple of years, but I came to learn something of desert people."

"Fascinating," he drawled. "I am dying to know what you learned about us in a couple of years."

"That when you swear vengeance on someone, you don't let up until your vow has been fulfilled."

"And my vow has not yet been satisfied, eh?"

"Would I be here?" she asked. "I'm not vain. I don't imagine that you were struck by my looks when I took rides in the desert. I'm not a beauty, like Princess Jamaila. I feel sure my hair is insipid beside her raven-dark hair. Her eyes are such a deep brown, her mouth a deep-red bow—how could I be any competition for someone so seductive?''

"Don't be too modest," he mocked. "There may not have been any mirrors at the convent school, but I feel sure there were a few at L'Oasis. You aren't as unaware of your-self as you pretend to be.''

She flung him a challenging look. "I know it pleases you to play games with me, Razul Bey, but I'm not as naive as you think.''

"Meaning?" He raised an eyebrow, something that could have been amusement in the depths of his eyes.

"If a man really wants a woman, he doesn't sit back and calmly smoke a cigar.''

"Ah, does that rankle with you, *ma petite*?''

"Not in the slightest." She scorned the very notion. "I was heartily glad when you let go of me. Being touched by you made my flesh crawl.''

Any sign of amusement vanished instantly from his eyes, leaving them like amber stones set in a golden mask. With a single lithe movement he was on his feet, pulling her up with him. He backed her to the parapet of the roof garden and tilted her into a back bend, so that her hair was streaming down toward the courtyard below.

"Shall I do it?" he asked in a dangerous voice. "Shall I be rid of you, as I am rid of Desirée, and close forever that insolent little mouth of yours? By Allah, I am tempted!''

As he tilted her farther over the wall, Lorne felt her legs leaving the ground. It was terrifying, like taking part in a dream over which she had no control, the stars dancing crazily in her eyes as she hung there in the bey's hands.

"You would smash to bits like a bird's egg dropped from a nest in a tree." He bit out the words. "My servants would have to scrape you off the flagstones—that makes you shudder, eh? Life is so sweet the moment it is threatened.''

With an abrupt movement he swung her clear of the wall and stood her upright, but he didn't remove his hands from her waist.

"Now you know what it feels like to have your flesh crawling," he said in a voice that matched the severe look he was giving her.

Lorne stood in his grasp, catching her breath and feeling as if her goose bumps would never deflate. Her mind was hung with an image of herself, suspended in space between his hands. Maybe her remark had been less than polite, but did he expect her to meekly accept his abduction of her to his palace, along with his tantalization of her, as if she were a toy with mechanical feelings?

"We hate the sight of each other, so why won't you let me go?" she asked, her gaze fixed upon a spray of stars beyond his broad shoulder.

"Have you not said it, *bint*?"

"Said—what?"

"That my vow of vengeance has not yet run its course."

"Yes, but surely I'm an innocent victim of the fight between you and Lion? I knew very little about L'Oasis, until I went to live there, and now I'm the whipping girl, the scapegoat, just because my mother's maiden name was Desirée. You know how Lion treated her, just because she fell in love with my father—he disowned her."

"Enough said." Razul Bey relaxed his grip on Lorne and moved away from her, leaning his back against the parapet where he had threatened her. "While it amuses me to keep you here in El Karah, I shall do so. When I grow tired of your company, you will be the first to know. And I beg of you—" he held up a hand "—don't inform me yet again that I am an insufferable bully and a libertine. I accept your definition of my character. I am a mogul who likes his own way—*Inshallah*."

Lorne drew in her breath as if to make a retort, then she let the words die on her lips. What was the use? Razul Kebîr had no regard for her as a person. He saw her only as a source of distraction, a blond doll whom he felt like playing with, as a big cat plays tormentingly with a mouse.

It only added to his amusement that she was a Desirée. It spiked his pleasure in bringing her to El Karah. Suddenly she wanted an end to the evening. She yearned to be alone.

"I—I want to go to bed—"

"Do you?"

He managed to make the words so insinuating that Lorne didn't know where to look. Her skin burned slowly, and then she heard him laugh—not a spontaneous, outright laugh, but his own special brand, starting deep in his throat, so that it emerged almost like a growl.

"An autocrat I might be, *ma femma*, but I don't commit rape. Your degradation isn't what I have in mind."

"Don't you think that I feel—degraded, being here like some slave object?" To her mortification the huskiness of tears was in her voice.

"Allow me to escort you to your bed," he said, without answering her question. "Come."

They traversed the winding stairway to the courtyard, where tiny flickering fireflies danced among the cypress trees, whose scent was potent on the night air. Lorne walked beside the bey, into the lamplit *serai*. The apprehensive drumming of her heart seemed to fill her eardrums. Oh God, what would he do now? She didn't trust him in the least, and she waited in dread to be flung to the luxury of the couch in its alcove of soft lamplight.

Razul Bey stood gazing around the bedchamber, taking in its seductive charm, the menace gone from his eyes so that they looked lambent. "I am thinking that a hotel room in Bar-Soudi would not be a quarter as commodious, nor as charming as this one. Don't you agree with me?"

Lorne was praying for him to take his leave. If he found the room too "charming," he might decide to stay the night, and that was the very last thing she wanted. "It's a little exotic for my taste," she replied. "You know very well that I'd prefer a hotel room to being here."

"Can't you think of yourself as my guest?" But he spoke with a touch of the sardonic in his voice.

"Do you usually force your hospitality upon people?" she rejoined, every inch of her as tense and as far removed from the bed as she could possibly get. The fine-spun drapings reminded her again of a net, and she didn't want to find herself entrapped in that net, in Razul Bey's muscular arms.

Her knees almost buckled when he took a step toward her, but it was her hand that he took hold of, holding its slimness in his strong fingers, the square fingernails so detailed against his brown skin. Lorne might possibly have admired such hands on any other man, but she was opposed to this one with every atom of her body. She could hardly bear to remember the way he had touched her up on the palace roof.

"You are shaking in your *babouches*," he mocked. "You can't wait for my departure, can you?"

"I—I'm very tired—"

"And you long to be alone, eh?"

"Yes." She kept her gaze fixed upon his hand holding hers, watching like a mesmerized rabbit confronted by a cobra, trying to stay calm as he slowly raised her hand to his lips and pressed them to her inner wrist. They were warm and almost as penetrating as a cobra sting.

"I thank you for an unusual evening," he said, his warm breath fanning her skin. "It came to me at L'Oasis, when we stood face-to-face for the first time, that you might prove to be—diverting."

Lorne wanted to snatch her hand from the warm brush of his mouth, but she restrained the impulse. Better to stay calm and indifferent, as if she didn't feel the almost electric tingle that ran up her arm and found its way along her collarbone.

She knew what his game was. Hadn't he said that he would make her aware of her own sensuality?

"I wish the sirocco had killed me," she said.

"No you don't, *femme blonde*. Life is good in any situation, and the adaptability of people is amazing. In a day or so you will become curious about your surroundings, and you may even find them fascinating."

"I doubt it," she asserted. "What prisoner ever liked its cage, and though the one I'm in might be gilded, it's still very much a cage."

Again he glanced around him, and this time his gaze dwelt on the wide, pavilioned, satin-covered bed. This time Lorne couldn't control the urge to snatch free of him; it happened in a flash, geared by her inability to trust him in the slightest degree. So far as Lorne was concerned, he was incapable of being anything but a libertine.

He watched as she backed away from him, her hands flexed to attack him if he came near her again. "You are being overdramatic, you know."

"I feel like a cat who's been pounced on by an oversized hound," she retorted. "Haven't you tantalized me enough for one evening? Surely there are women in your *serai* who are panting for your attentions?"

"Doubtless," he drawled.

Lorne damned with a look every inch of his easy grace in the Eastern clothing, which intensified his barbarous good looks. "I suppose you find them too willing?" she said. "You prefer tormenting me, don't you? Well, I'll fight you every inch of the way, and that's a promise."

"Is it, really?" A smile curled the edge of his mouth. "Has it not occurred to you, *mon chou*, that if you were less reluctant, I might soon tire of the game?"

She flung him a scornful look. "You know I'll never throw myself at you, like other women. I'm not fooled by your manly appearance or your position of leadership. I see right through you, my lord. I see a man without honor!"

This time she had hit a nerve, for his eyes flashed with a deadly brilliance, transfixing her on their golden steel. "So, my little antagonist, it is going to be a lengthy siege, eh?"

"It looks that way," she agreed.

"And our encounters will be explosive?"

"They are bound to be."

"We may become addicted to our battles. They may hold us together, while your surrender might push us apart. Will you risk it?"

"I have no other option, Lord Razul. I could never give in to you of my own free will."

As they stood facing each other, the bedchamber lamps emitted a spicy scent, not strong but constant. In this room, with its muted lamplight and opulent barbarity, the bey looked utterly at home, but Lorne despised it all and wished herself in the plainest of rooms, with whitewashed walls and a narrow bed, such as the one she had slept in at the convent school.

She was a free soul who wanted her liberty and the right to choose her companionship.

"I'll never—never give in to you," she exclaimed. Her eyes were densely blue as they dwelt on the inflexibility of his shoulders, then lifted to the hard force of his chin. He had a quality of stillness as he stood there, like the desert itself. A stillness with a diabolical quality, because at any second it might become an overpowering force that could sweep her right off her feet.

He regarded her with a barbaric detachment from her feelings. A man to whom a woman was no more than a—a pleasure garden. She must have read that somewhere, perhaps in one of the books that, like everything else, had burned to ashes at L'Oasis—her life there, and her belief that, at last, she was part of someone who cared about her.

Even that was gone, snatched away from her by Razul Kebîr. He had left her with nothing but the will to fight him, and she tilted her chin and pressed her lips into a stubborn line.

He carried a brown hand to his forehead, then touched it to his lips and breast. "This was written."

As she stood there mutely, he turned on his heel and left her alone at last.

For moments on end Lorne didn't move, unable to believe that he wouldn't suddenly return to the bedchamber. When all at once the bead curtain rattled, she almost jumped out of her skin. But it was Kasha who entered.

"The *lel-lah* is tired and wishes to go to bed." Kasha spoke as if instructed. "I am here to assist—"

"No," Lorne broke in. "I can manage on my own. You go to your bed, Kasha."

"I can't do so, *lel-lah*, until you are settled. His Eminence would be displeased."

"He won't know." Lorne pushed distractedly at her hair, looking around as if for a means of escape and finding none.

"My Lord Razul is in conversation with his guards, and he would notice if I returned too soon to my own apartment." Kasha approached Lorne. "Permit me to assist you in your disrobing."

Lorne gave in, for she certainly didn't want Kasha to get into trouble. She knew only too well how formidable Razul Bey could be, and it was only natural that members of his staff would prefer to carry out his instructions rather than disobey them.

She submitted to Kasha's ministrations, shivering with an emotional coldness when the beaded tunic was removed. Then she heard a catch of breath and saw that Kasha was staring at the diamond she wore, glittering with blue fire against her skin. It felt like a stone, a lump of ice against Lorne's body, and she drew the chain over her head and dropped the pendant to a table.

She turned to where a silver washbowl was placed in readiness, dashing rose water over her skin before putting on the diaphanous night toga laid out on the bed. This was in a primrose color, of a fabric so sensuously fine that it embarrassed Lorne. She felt as if every single item in the *serai* was designed to make her aware of herself.

Kasha's glance at the diamond pendant had spoken volumes, but Lorne refused to mention it as she sat silent on one of the huge, supple leather cushions, unable to stop brooding on the events of the evening as Kasha kneeled and brushed her hair. The hairbrush had a matching comb of tortoiseshell inlaid with pearl. Every item in the room was felicitous and, with all her soul, Lorne wanted to deny the beauty of her surroundings.

She sighed. It wasn't in her nature to deny beauty when she saw it, and all of this was incredibly real. None of it was the figment of a dream, no more than the feel of the tortoiseshell brush as Kasha drew it in long strokes through her hair.

"The *lel-lah* sighs deeply," Kasha murmured. "Yet in your possession you have a diamond worth very much, which must mean that the Lord Razul is pleased with you."

Lorne flushed at the implication in the words. Did Kasha suppose that she had been paid for services rendered up there on the starlit ramparts of the palace?

"He's rich," she said icily. "I expect he gives away diamonds as if they're candy bars. I wonder, Kasha, would one of his loyal subjects dare to help me get away from him?"

"The *lel-lah* still wishes to go?"

"With all my heart!" Lorne surged to her bare feet and began to pace up and down the room on the lush carpets underfoot. "Oh, what wouldn't I give.... Do you suppose there is anyone who would dare to help me?"

"It would take a lot of daring," Kasha murmured as she put away the gold chains that she had removed from Lorne's hair.

Lorne swung to look at her, her body showing tense through the night toga. "There has to be someone in El Karah who isn't afraid of the mighty bey, nor so besotted by his aura that treating his actions as godlike is the normal procedure. Believe me, I would keep it secret, if only some-one could be found!"

"Our people love a secret." Kasha was turning down the bed, with its big downy pillows and the silk-soft linen under the tawny throw. "That is why he likes to keep his women in *purdah*."

"Don't you mean purgatory?" Lorne exclaimed.

"Come to your bed, *lel-lah*. Sleep and forget your trou-bles."

Kasha was right, of course. Only when she slept would she be at rest for a while from her troubled fears and hopes. She came to the bed and slid beneath the covers. At the end of an active day, bed had been a haven. Now it had become a hazardous place that the bey of Karah could invade, with his strong, brazen-skinned body and his brown and know-ing hands.

Lorne pulled the covers to her chin, as if to protect her-self, as a child will if it sees a spider on the wall. That was how starkly Razul Bey's face was engraved on her mind. Every nuance of his voice was indelible.

"You don't really understand my feelings, do you, Ka-sha?" She gazed up wistfully at the woman whose kindness was her only link with the world beyond the palace walls, where she hadn't known what it was like to fear a man's in-tentions.

Kasha studied Lorne's silvery-gold hair against the pil-lows. "You are a *roumia* and our ways are strange to you. Given time—"

"No!" Lorne protested. "I won't be told that in time I shall accept being here. I never shall! Oh, I know what you're thinking. Who eats the bey's bread, sings his tune, but I won't! I—I'm not a person while I stay here. I'm just an addition to his other goods and chattels—his other women! They might thrill to a man who expects a woman to kiss the hand he abducts her with, but I consider him beneath contempt."

"Hush." Kasha put a hand to her lips. "Rest. Rest and sleep."

"Sleep!" Lorne echoed. "In my state of mind?"

"It will come, *lel-lah*," Kasha promised.

Lorne lay in the dimness of the big room, where a single lamp had been turned down low. Kasha had left lime cordial at her bedside, in a cup lidded with gilt flowers, along with sugared biscuits and cubes of fruit jelly. She had everything she could possibly require; she lay in a bed of total comfort, like the indulged favorite of the *pasha*, and she might as well have been lying on a bed of nails.

Every moment she had spent with Razul Bey was imprinted on her mind; every word he had spoken still echoed in her ears. She could still envision his face when he had leaned over her and unbuttoned with teasing slowness her beaded tunic. He had looked at her as if he owned every portion of her body. He had ravished her with his eyes, and she curled into a ball at the memory of it.

She could hear him saying yet again, "There are many names of the desert—some have called it the garden of desire."

She remembered the way he had pinched the air with his fingers, when emphasizing a statement. Never, never would she bow to his hand!

The scenes slid through her mind to the accompaniment of a lamp chain tinkling in a slight breeze, or the soft rattle of beads at the doorway. And through the lacy wood screens of the windows there stole the husky music of countless cicadas in the palm trees.

"I hate him—hate this place..." Lorne whispered to her pillow.

Big eyed, she lay there, in the midst of Eastern luxury. Of furniture with a silken dark patina, black almost as ebony, with ivory and pearl inlays. The lamp burned low on an inlaid chest, arabesqued in silver. There was a glimmer of pearly bowls of face powder and kohl, and long-necked bottles of toilet water.

She wanted for nothing—except her freedom.

Flinging an arm around a pillow, she hugged it to her, rather like a child seeking comfort from a bewildering change in its life. She had a silken, barbarous captivity in place of her freedom. Diamonds and desire in place of being a person who could make her own choices. Her fingernails bit deep into the pillow, as if it had turned into the threatening shoulder of her captor.

Sleep would only come if she could think of other people, other days, so that the images of the bey were put out of focus.

Desperately Lorne sought relief from his lingering touch and the things he had said to her. With all her will she turned back her thoughts to her school days, walking in a crocodile—single file—with the other girls, giggling at innocuous secrets, wondering in whispers what life held in store for them.

"Stop chattering," the Sister in charge would order. "Behave like young ladies and don't shuffle along."

One of Lorne's friends had decided to be a nurse, and for a time Lorne had felt an inclination to do the necessary training. Then had come that unexpected invitation from Lionel Desirée, her grandfather who lived in fascinating El Karah.

El Karah of the golden kings, the green oases and the timeless desert. She knew instinctively that to visit El Karah was to step backward into history, where strange and haunting things had occurred. Across the sands of El Karah had driven the war chariots of the rulers of one of the earliest civilizations, a lovely, unique place that Lorne couldn't resist.

When Lion found the time, he had taken her to see an ancient burial monument, and there on a staircase she had seen a fresco of a former king, his pet lion beside him.

Lorne shivered and pressed herself into her pillow, and once again there was no shutting out the face that had drawn so close to her own, as detailed as the face of a sun god.

CHAPTER SIX

FOR A SUCCESSION OF DAYS Lorne didn't see hide nor hair of Razul Bey, and she learned from Kasha that he had duties elsewhere and might be away from El Karah for an indefinite time.

Lorne breathed a sigh of relief, but soon discovered that she was still under surveillance by his guards, who followed at a discreet pace when she strolled in the palace grounds.

Though it was cooler inside the *serai*, out of the sun that burned so white against the palace walls, Lorne had discovered a terrace of gardens, each one below the other, and she felt more at ease among the trees and flowers than she did inside the luxury of her prison.

With Razul Bey away from his domain, her thoughts turned constantly to thoughts of getting away from El Karah before he returned. She hoped that his staff would be less observant of her and pleaded with Kasha to find someone who would supply her with a horse, and perhaps guide her to Bar-Soudi.

"The anger of His Eminence would stretch across the sands like a rock shadow when the sun goes down," Kasha replied.

"But you said I might be able to buy my freedom, and I have the diamond."

"You must give me time," Kasha said. "These things are not done in a day."

"Time!" Lorne exclaimed. "It seems as if time has never moved forward in this place—as if it has stood still for five hundred years. I don't belong here! I have to return to my kind of life!''

Kasha seemed to agree, but she begged Lorne to have patience.

"Is everyone afraid of one man?" Lorne demanded from where she sat in a window seat with her legs curled under her.

"That one man is the bey of Karah, and ever since the start of his regime he has proved his authority and his fairness in dealing with people."

"Fairness?" Lorne looked disgusted. "He's about as fair-minded as a rattlesnake. He doesn't know the meaning of the word. All he cares about is his sense of power over people. When he shows a little patronage, they feel flattered by him. When he frowns they run for cover. He's a tyrant!"

"You see it that way because you are not one of us, *lellah*." The look that Kasha gave Lorne was like that of a mother trying to deal with the tantrum of a child. "We know of his good works, and there are girls who would be only too happy to be in your place.''

"They're welcome," Lorne retorted. "I wasn't brought up to regard men as my rod and comfort, and the light of my existence. I can manage perfectly well without being bossed about by the mighty Razul Bey. It's a relief not to have him striding in here as if he's my—''

Lorne broke off, biting her lip. Then she jumped to her feet and in flight from her thoughts she hurried from the *serai*, swirling about her head the muslin, which kept the sun from giving her a splitting headache. She ran down a flight of stone steps, making for the garden of turtles, huge, friendly creatures with magnificent shells of muted gold, brown and black. When she spoke to them, they actually came to her to be stroked.

She was petting one of them when she became aware of being watched from under a palm tree, whose enormous leaves hung like a parasol above the figure of Princess Ja-

maila. Then the princess moved away from the shady tree
and came toward Lorne, bringing with her the clink of golden jewelry.

"I have heard that the English show more feeling toward
animals than they show toward each other." Her almond-
shaped eyes slid over Lorne as she spoke, taking in her leg-
hugging pants, the sandals and plain tunic that made her
look boyish. The dark crescents of her eyebrows rose in a
statement that Lorne instantly read. The princess thought
her a very odd addition to the bey's household.

"Yes, we are fond of animals," she agreed. "You can
trust their loyalty rather more than you can trust that of
human beings."

"Would you say the same of a tiger?" The princess spoke
with a hint of mockery in her voice.

"Not if you're referring to Razul Bey." Lorne didn't
hesitate to let the other girl know that she, too had likened
him to that proud and dangerous creature.

"You should never question the loyalty of our people. We
abide by our word as you of the West often fail to do. Our
tribal and family links are forged of a steel that rarely bends
in a wind of change—such as the sirocco that brought you
here."

"It was no wind," Lorne retaliated. "It was a man, and
I feel certain everyone knows that I didn't come willingly to
El Karah. He tricked me. He made me believe that he was
taking me to Bar-Soudi."

"So you don't like being here?"

"I'd be out of here like a shot, if those two guards weren't
always on my heels. I'd take my chance—"

"In the desert, rather than in the arms of a man so powerful and handsome?"

Lorne's heart gave a tempestuous beat, for the words
conjured up images she was desperate to forget. "I want to
get away. Would you help me?"

"I could be persuaded to help you." The princess admired a gold bracelet on her dusky-gold arm. "There is something of Razul Bey's that I should like to have—"

"I'll do anything," Lorne said eagerly. "Just tell me what you want."

"It's a velvet box." The slim, hennaed hands described its oblong shape. "Inside there is a fan, adorned with rubies and diamonds on the handle. It belonged to his—to my aunt. I should have come by it, but Razul keeps it locked away in a chest, to which he alone has the key."

The princess looked intently at Lorne. "I see the doubt in your eyes, but in that chest there is Western clothing—outmoded it's true, but the kind you would prefer to wear."

"Western clothing?" Lorne looked astonished.

"The aunt I speak of was French. She was traveling in the desert with her husband, and one evening their encampment was set upon, possibly by a band of nomads. They were left for dead, but the following morning a troop of cavalrymen came upon the site, and it was discovered that the beautiful Frenchwoman was still breathing and still clutched in her hand was the fan, which the nomads had overlooked in their haste to plunder the tents. She was carried to El Karah, which was then governed by my grandfather, the Prince Kemel Kebîr. The *cavalerie de charge* had given orders that her scattered clothing be gathered up and placed in an abandoned chest, and this was also brought to the palace."

"What of her husband?" Lorne murmured.

"He and the servants were buried in the desert." The princess spread her hands significantly. "She had been struck over the head and suffered a concussion, which blanked out her memory for a considerable time. In that interval my grandfather's brother became fond of her and requested that she remain with him in El Karah. The prince gave his consent to their marriage, and in time she produced a son. The child was less than a year old when she took sick and died, for she had never fully recovered from her injury."

Princess Jamaila paused, and the silence was filled with a message, which made Lorne open wide her eyes in incredulity. "She was the mother of Razul Kebîr?"

"Exactement."

"Then how can you say that the jeweled fan should be yours?"

A sudden look of petulance passed across the lovely face. "I was shown the fan when I was about twelve years old, and ever since I have wanted it for my own. Many times I've tried to coax it out of Razul. He never gives me a definite answer, and there it lies among those fading garments, still with sand on them. I have said to my cousin's face that he isn't a man of sentiment, and he has agreed with me, smiling in that ironic way of his. The fan means little to him. His mother died before he could really know her—"

"That may not be true," Lorne broke in. "During the first months of its life a baby is with the mother day and night, and a bond is naturally forged. If the mother dies, then the bond is cruelly broken. The boy cries and frets for her, but she doesn't return, and despite what you say about his lack of sentiment, Razul Bey might have deep-seated memories of the mother he loved and lost, and the fan may mean more to him than he cares to admit."

"You say that because you don't really know him."

"I've no wish to know him," Lorne was quick to reply. "And I don't see how I can get hold of the fan if he keeps it locked away."

"A woman has ways and means," the princess said insinuatingly. "At the present time you are privy to his private life, and a man abandons his clothing when he goes to bed."

Lorne flushed to the roots of her hair. "If you're implying that I can go hunting for keys in his pockets, then you're mistaken. I don't—sleep with the man!"

"If you wish my help in getting away from El Karah, then you will have to find a way to get that chest open." The brown eyes upon Lorne were less than gazellelike. "I want the fan. I shall have it."

"You talk like a spoiled child," Lorne said in exasperation. "It would be stealing—"

"You could ask him to give it to you, then you could give it to me. For some curious reason he wishes to have you in his bed. Why else would he bring you to the palace?"

"I—I'm sure I don't know." Lorne's flush still lingered.

"Are you afraid of his attentions?" The Princess Jamaila looked inquisitive. "Are you a virgin?"

"That's none of your business—"

"But it's true!" The brown eyes flashed over Lorne. "You could get me the fan without any trouble at all. If Razul wishes to take your innocence, then you could ask anything of him. Don't you realize it, you little fool of a *roumia*?"

"I—I'll ask him for nothing."

"I thought you wanted, above all, to get away from him?"

"I won't—can't stoop to what you're suggesting. I'm neither a fancy woman, nor a petty thief."

"You are noble, eh?" The princess smiled maliciously. "You are going to suffer in silence, eh?"

"If I have to." But Lorne spoke with more nerve than conviction.

"It is the British way?"

"I—I suppose it is."

"What a pity, because it would be quite easy for me to get you a horse. I could provide you with a compass and set you in the right direction for Bar-Soudi, and water for the journey could also be yours for the asking. You could be gone from El Karah before my cousin returns to the palace."

As these temptations were listed, Lorne felt herself weakening. "But you spoke of a key. He probably keeps it on his person."

"You could break the lock—ah, couldn't you do that? Would it be such a black mark against your British character?"

"If you're so eager to own the fan, then why not break the lock yourself?"

"Because I couldn't pass his guards in order to enter his apartment, but no such restraint would be imposed upon you—his *kadin*."

Lorne's eyes lit up with indignation. "That's what everyone imagines! That I'm his mistress. That's what Razul Bey has made it seem, but it doesn't happen to be true!"

"Really? We are a subtle people, but we are simplicity itself when it comes to a man and a woman. Yes, in bringing you to his *serai*, my cousin Razul has let it be known that you are fancied by him. You can come and go as you desire, within the constraints of the *serai*. If you entered his apartment, his guards would take little notice. Despite what you may think, the woman of the East is often spoiled and indulged beyond what you experience in the West, where the women struggle to be as virile as the men. We are born woman or man, and each has a special kind of power. The woman who tries to be a man is a freak, and the man who tries to be a woman is a fool. The simple way is to feel at ease in one's own skin."

The Princess Jamaila smiled, as if she found enormous pleasure in her own dusky-gold skin. "You pine for your Western way of life, so let me help you to return."

"At a price, of course." Inwardly Lorne was seething, all her rage against Razul Bey having risen to boiling point. She'd show him what he could do with his favors.... Let him give them to one of his swooning Eastern girls.

"There is always a price to pay," the princess agreed. "That is the way of life, East or West."

"No jeweled fan, no horse for me?" Lorne's eyes were painfully blue in her white face. "All right, I'll get you the fan, if it means so much to you."

"It is *très jolie*." The princess laughed with delight. "You will bring it to me—here. I think, tomorrow at this time. And tomorrow evening you will have your horse and enough food and water to last you on your journey. You know, you are a puzzlement."

"Why so?"

"You can't wait to get away from a man who has much power, much sway over the province. There are women who would be highly delighted to be in his hands."

"Meaning yourself?" Lorne asked coldly.

The almond-shaped eyes narrowed to slits. "How dare you speak in that manner to me?"

"Why, have I struck a nerve?"

"I am of a higher station in life than you."

"So elevated, Princess Jamaila, that you ask me to steal for you."

"Merely because Razul is obstinate about giving me the fan." The princess moved one of her hennaed hands, as if already she felt the jeweled handle in her clasp. "I am his closest female relative, and the fan should be mine. What would he do with it?"

"Give it, perhaps, to his *kadin*," Lorne said with the deliberate intention of jolting the vanity of Razul Bey's cousin.

"He would not give something so precious to a paramour." The narrowed eyes raked Lorne from head to heel. "You are wise to get away from a man who would use you for his pleasure, then cast you aside. You are, after all, only a passing fancy for the bey, who will take for his wife a lovely, delicate, well-bred Eastern girl. There is one such spoken of, but at present she is only fourteen years old, and Razul will probably wait for her to become sixteen. By then she will be even lovelier, and tutored in the ways of pleasing a man."

The princess allowed her words to sink into Lorne's mind, where they twisted and writhed and intensified her need to get away from him.

"Such tutoring is ignored in the West, is this not so? Especially within the stone walls of a convent school."

"Our ways are as different from yours as chalk and cheese," Lorne agreed, while her mind still burned with images of herself, subjected to Razul Bey's attentions even as he waited for his future bride to mature. "The people of El Karah are not only ruthless, they are less than civilized. We allow English girls to grow up before subjecting them to the baser facts of life."

"Perhaps your lack of wisdom in such matters is the cause of your fright where Razul is concerned. It isn't unknown for a girl to get rich during the time she is favored by a wealthy man. Do you prefer to be poor?"

"I prefer to be free." It was a cry from the heart, for anything was preferable to being the object of a man's pleasure—a *fille de joie*, to be paid off with jewelry. Lorne felt insulted by the very thought, the simplicity of a convent upbringing at the root of her being.

"Razul Bey doesn't frighten me," she denied. "I imagine it's in the nature of an overlord to make his own rules, but it isn't in my nature to submit to them. I abominate him!"

The Princess Jamaila raised a slender, taunting eyebrow. "Then it is best that you go. Otherwise, he will make you obey his slightest wish. Ah, you are foolish if you believe he can't do this, to any woman. He's a man among men; otherwise one of my brothers would be in his boots. He takes command with the lifting of a finger, and that is the way it is among people of the East. Being born in the right bed doesn't guarantee the right to the cords of office. Fools are often born in a privileged bed, and Razul was chosen to be the bey, which makes him even more important."

"Autocratic." Lorne's features were as if carved in ice, her eyes flashing diamond blue. "High and mighty, and sure of himself. Ruthless as a demon and tough as oxen leather. He was quite unmoved when he found me alone, in a storm-damaged house, with the dead body of my grandfather. He decided that it might be amusing to make a slut out of me. I hate every arrogant inch of him! I—I'd like to make him feel as unhappy as I do, but he's as hard as nails, and nothing could ever dent his intolerable ego. It would deflect a well-aimed knife!"

"You hate him with such passion," murmured the princess. "I believe you would kill him if you had the weapon."

"I would." Lorne spoke recklessly. "I'd like to see him in hell."

"Razul is a man. He believes that paradise awaits him when he dies."

"Naturally." Lorne gave a scornful toss of her head. "It seems to me that the Eastern way of life is entirely in favor of the man. What does a woman get out of it?"

Once again Princess Jamaila admired the band of gold that encircled her arm. "If a woman is wise, she gets as much jewelry as she can wear. Should she fall out of favor, the jewelry remains hers to keep. If a man dared to retain it, then she could ask her brothers to deal with him."

Lorne couldn't control a shudder. She had found out with a vengeance that time stood still in the desert, where the old customs were still very much alive. By bringing her to El Karah, the bey had made her a participant, and if she was to elude him, then she must use ways and means that once would have been unthinkable.

Everything had its price, and she must pay it, if she wanted to get out of Razul Kebîr's hands. Those strong brown hands, with their sensual awareness of a woman's body.... As a current of memory ran through Lorne, she decided that she must get away before Razul Bey returned and came looking for her in the *serai*. She'd do anything rather than have him touch her—ever again.

"Between a man and a woman," said the princess, "it is a kind of duel. There are those who enjoy every cut and thrust, every loss and every gain." She considered Lorne, amusedly. "It's amazing that my Lord Razul should bring to his palace a girl who would feel happier in the cloisters of a nunnery. I am right, yes?"

Lorne gave a shrug, remembering how she had longed to escape the restrictions of the convent school. "Anything would be preferable," she replied.

"How strange of you, to prefer the veil of a nun to the seven veils of love."

"I thought it was a dance." Lorne tried to look indifferent.

"As the dancer slowly discards her veils until she is fully revealed, so it is with two people. The reluctance to release the first veil, and perhaps the second veil, until the shyness becomes sensuous and the unveiling becomes eager, until at last the heart has nothing more to hide."

The princess moved her hands in the delicate gestures of a dancer. "My people know that love does not come with a single glance, as you of the West sing of it in your songs. Perhaps you of the West become unhappy because you make the mistake of believing that love happens like a flash of lightning. A meeting of eyes, and suddenly there is a vista of heaven on earth."

She laughed, and her Eastern eyes were deep and knowing. "Our desert culture is supposed to be less civilized than your own, but the truth is that we have held on to our wisdom, which we know to have its roots in the primitive beginning of things. In all the years, have the stars in the sky changed their color? Has the moon risen at noon and the sun at midnight? So it is between a man and a woman, as it was at the beginning—a duel of the senses, a dance of the seven veils."

Lorne couldn't argue with the Princess Jamaila on such a subject. What did she know of love? At the convent school it had been a forbidden subject, to talk of the things that took place between a man and a woman. Emphasis had been placed upon the spiritual side of life. The pupils had been encouraged to believe in a heavenly joy rather than a physical one. They had been taught that the body was only a tool, to be put to use but never enjoyed—least of all in a covering of sensuous veils.

As these thoughts went through Lorne's mind, she became aware that the princess was studying her in a curious way. "Do you like dressing as a boy?" she asked.

"Oh—these?" Lorne half smiled and touched a hand to her tunic and *sirwals*, her leg-hugging pants. "I needed daytime clothing, and these seemed more appropriate than the clothing I'm given to wear in the evening. Perhaps I am something of a tomboy, for I don't feel at ease in gauzy silks and satins."

"What will you do when you arrive at Bar-Soudi?"

"Be terribly relieved." Lorne spoke from the heart. "You won't let me down, will you?"

"Not if you obtain the fan."

"Won't Razul Bey be fearfully angry when he finds you have it?"

"I shall keep it hidden from him, and he'll believe that you stole it for yourself."

Lorne flinched from the barefaced reply. She felt a sense of recoil but realized that he was bound to think of her as the thief who had broken into the chest, in which lay his memories of his mother. She didn't want to go through with her side of the bargain, but at the same time she couldn't remain here. With every bit of herself she wanted to be gone from El Karah by the time Razul Bey came riding back from wherever he had been, no doubt cracking the whip of authority.

"Being unscrupulous must run in your family." Lorne spoke with a cold dislike of both the Princess Jamaila and the part she must play if she was to get free of Razul Kebîr. Anything was preferable, even the casting aside of principles that had been schooled into her, taking root as lessons do when a child has learned them from an early age.

"We are merely sure of what we want from life." The princess smiled with a touch of disdain. "It is called determination, and surely you have seen it stamped into the face of my cousin? There are times when scruples have to be brushed aside like webs in a room rarely used, and this you and I will do, *roumia*, in order to obtain what we want. I am sure your Jesuit saints won't strike you down with an avenging sword."

In Lorne's mind it was more like a scimitar, a gleaming sword of the East, that swung above her head all the time she remained in the palace of the bey. It was the seductive threat in the voice of a man that hung over her, in ever-descending arcs of silken-steel desire, causing her hands to clench until her fingernails dug into her flesh. Instincts were warning her not to be available to the bey when he returned to El Karah.

Whatever of France was in his veins had long been diluted by the Eastern side of his nature. His mother had died too soon to teach him some of her European ways. Instead, he had grown up to be wholly a man of El Karah, a seeker of power in an environment where women were beings of pleasure and recreation, their main value to a man their ability to bear his children.

"So he's waiting for his future wife to grow up?" Lorne forced herself to speak the words. "And while he waits, he thinks he can enjoy himself with me! I despise him for his selfish arrogance!"

The princess shrugged her silk-clad shoulders. "You despise what other women admire. You want no dealings with a man among men. There are many who would call you a fool among women.''

"I daresay there are.'' Lorne ran her gaze around the garden of turtles, feeling as if her spirit was as weighed down as the turtles beneath the great shields on their backs. "I won't be the plaything of any man—least of all a man who thinks his looks and power give him the right to treat women any way he pleases. Good luck to those who think he's bestowing some kind of an honor upon them. I have another word for it.''

Lorne shivered hot and cold, and suddenly she wanted to be alone, alone in the cool dimness of the *serai*, with a cup of coffee to help soothe her unsettled feelings.

"I'll get you the jeweled fan.'' Her eyes were fixed, icily blue upon the face of Princess Jamaila. "But if you don't keep your side of the bargain, then I shall repeat every word of this conversation to your cousin. I don't think you'd like him to know how avaricious you are.''

"You have my word,'' the princess said haughtily. "I suppose you can manage an Arabian horse?''

"The horse I lost in the storm was an Arabian.'' Lorne thought sadly of Firefly.... Everything had been lost in the winds of storm, and she felt afraid of nothing except a man in a flowing cloak, his eyes tiger gold in a face whose attraction was more terrible than thoughts of the desert and its changing moods.

"This time tomorrow, then.'' She turned and left the princess on her own, a figure of outward grace but inwardly a person with a devious mind, probably spoiled from childhood and determined to have whatever she desired.

A jeweled fan! Lorne ran as if chased by the thought, up the stone steps that led to another of the palace gardens, this one rampant with rosebushes in every imaginable color. Huge, glorious blooms, and others so compact that they looked like buds among the leaves. Lorne paused in front of a bush of sheerest pink roses, exquisitely formed and with-

. . . be tempted!

See inside for special
4 FREE BOOKS offer

Harlequin Presents®

Discover deliciously different romance with 4 Free Novels from

Harlequin Presents·

Sit back and enjoy four exciting romances—yours **FREE** from Harlequin Reader Service! But wait . . . there's *even more* to this great offer!

HARLEQUIN FOLDING UMBRELLA— ABSOLUTELY FREE! You'll love your Harlequin umbrella. Its bright color will cheer you up on even the gloomiest day. It's made of rugged nylon to last for years and is so compact (folds to 15″) you can carry it in your purse or briefcase. This folding umbrella is yours free with this offer!

PLUS A FREE MYSTERY GIFT—a surprise bonus that will delight you!

All this just for trying our Reader Service!

MONEY-SAVING HOME DELIVERY!

Once you receive your 4 FREE books and gifts, you'll be able to preview more great romance reading in the convenience of your own home at less than retail prices. Every month we'll deliver 8 brand-new Harlequin Presents novels right to your door months before they appear in stores. If you decide to keep them, they'll be yours for only $1.99 each! That's .26¢ less per book than what you pay in stores—with no additional charges for home delivery.

SPECIAL EXTRAS—FREE!

You'll also get our newsletter with each shipment, packed with news of your favorite authors and upcoming books— FREE! And as a valued reader, we'll be sending you additional free gifts from time to time—as a token of our appreciation.

BE TEMPTED! COMPLETE, DETACH AND MAIL YOUR POSTPAID ORDER CARD TODAY AND RECEIVE 4 FREE BOOKS, A FOLDING UMBRELLA AND MYSTERY GIFT—PLUS LOTS MORE!

A FREE
Folding Umbrella

and Mystery Gift *await you, too!*

Harlequin Presents®

Harlequin Reader Service®
901 Fuhrmann Blvd., P.O. Box 1394, Buffalo, NY 14240-9963

☐ **YES!** Please rush me my four Harlequin Presents novels with my FREE Folding Umbrella and Mystery Gift. As explained on the opposite page, I understand that I am under no obligation to purchase any books. The free books and gifts remain mine to keep.

108 CIP CAMG

NAME _____ (please print)

ADDRESS _____ APT. _____

CITY _____ STATE _____ ZIP CODE _____

Offer limited to one per household and not valid for present subscribers. Prices subject to change.

HARLEQUIN READER SERVICE "NO-RISK" GUARANTEE

- There's no obligation to buy—and the free books and gifts remain yours to keep.
- You pay the lowest price possible and receive books before they appear in stores.
- You may end your subscription anytime—just write and let us know.

If offer card is missing, write to: Harlequin Reader Service, 901 Fuhrmann Blvd., P.O. Box 1394, Buffalo, NY 14240-1394.

out a thorn on their stems. She gently broke a stem and carried the rose into the *serai*, holding it to her nostrils and letting it waft her back to the English countryside.

It was true, after all. Few people counted their blessings until they were lost, and it was hopeless to wish that she had never seen the desert, never felt the rush of excitement that had carried her away from the security of the convent school into realms of gold, sadly tarnished by the storm.

The sirocco, which had left her bereft of Lion . . . the bey who had snatched away the veils of illusion and left her to face the naked truth of why she had been invited to L'Oasis.

She sank down on a big floor cushion and unfurled her turban. Her hair fell in glistening disarray around her pensive face, tumbling into its natural wave above her shadowed eyes. She was trapped in a cage, and there was only one way to break out of it. She had to become a thief!

"Will the *lel-lah* take coffee?" Kasha had entered the room in her silent-footed way.

"Can you get me a horse?" Lorne asked the question, but she already knew the reply.

"I have told the *lel-lah*, these things take time."

"Time and caution." Lorne set her lips in resolve. It was no use relying on Kasha's help. She was a servant in the palace, but the Princess Jamaila was Razul's cousin and couldn't be punished with dismissal.

"Yes, I will have a cup of coffee."

"With cakes, those almond-cream slices that you like?"

"Yes, why not?"

Kasha frowned slightly as she studied Lorne, who was sniffing the pink rose as if it were a drug. "Shall I ask Ali to cut you a bunch of roses?"

Lorne slowly shook her head. "I stole only one. The rest of the roses look lovelier where they are. It isn't always kind, Kasha, to take a rose, or a person, out of its natural environment. You see, this one is already drooping."

"It needs water," Kasha said, a sudden touch of concern in her voice as she studied Lorne. "Is the *lel-lah* feeling quite well? You covered your head from the sun?"

"I haven't got sunstroke." Lorne stroked the rose against her cheekbone. "Do I seem light-headed?"

"Yes."

Lorne smiled cynically. "Have you had orders to keep the bey's *kadin* in good condition?" She raised her eyes to Kasha's face and saw from the woman's expression that she had been given such an order. "If my spirit droops, don't you think there is just cause? Why do all of you act as if I have something to sing about? Singing doesn't come naturally to a caged bird."

"Often a bird in a cage is safer than a bird on the wind, where the hawks and eagles fly."

"Not to mention the vultures." Lorne spoke with a meaningful note in her voice. "I'm not safe in *his* cage, Kasha! I'm behind bars, even if they are made of silk!"

Lorne looked around the magnificent room, remembering how Razul Bey had filled its every corner with the aura of his personality. Her fingers crushed the rose, unaware, and something inside her weakened at the very thought of Razul Kebîr. He cast his powerful shadow even when he was absent from El Karah, and she knew there was only one course she could take in order to flee him . . . down the corridors of her mind, and across the desert sands to where he couldn't touch her anymore.

Now she noticed the ruined rose and let it fall to the floor. It lay there broken, as if it symbolized her own fate. And at this defeatist thought, she thrust up her chin and pushed the hair from her brow.

She'd do what she had to do—she'd do it this evening and to the devil with scruples. As the princess had said, they sometimes had to be swept aside like cobwebs in a room rarely used.

Like the *kadin* he had left all on her own, she would go to
his apartment, and they'd think she was a lovesick woman
who sought his aura and his scent in place of his arms. It
would never occur to his guards to believe otherwise. They
saw him as an admirable figure of a man, who donated a
great honor upon the woman he took for his pleasure.

Her lips twisted with scorn. She'd show the almighty one
just what she thought of him!

"Thank you." She accepted coffee and cakes from Kasha, and now that she had made up her mind about the
evening ahead, Lorne felt more relaxed. She stretched out
on the couch and sipped her coffee, but her air of brooding
wasn't lost on her maid.

"Can't you be content, *lel-lah*?" she asked. "Your every
need is attended to. Your smallest desire is granted."

"Is it?" Lorne murmured. "Kasha, if I had been raised
to this kind of life, then I would settle for it. But where I
come from, a girl has a choice in the matter of..." The
words faded on her lips, they were such potent, image-
forming words. "Oh—you know what I mean."

"You speak of being loved."

"Love is a curious word for it." Lorne's smile was fleeting. "There isn't much of that in what Razul Bey feels for
me. He fancies me, and he also feels like taking me down a
few pegs because I'm a Desirée. You would think he would
like French people, wouldn't you?"

Kasha didn't rise to the bait, so Lorne shrugged her
shoulders and helped herself to a cake. In a little while the
bead curtain rattled as the maid withdrew from the room,
leaving Lorne to reflect on the Frenchwoman who had lived
just long enough to bring Razul Bey into the world.

And tonight... A shiver of anticipation ran through
Lorne. Tonight she would touch the clothing and com-
mune in a strange way with the woman who had produced
such an arrogant devil of a son.

CHAPTER SEVEN

THE COURTYARD WAS star-shadowed, the scents of flowered vines potent on the night air. Wrapped in a hooded cloak, Lorne crossed to the arcade, which led into the apartments of Razul Bey. The mystery of the night was more appealing to her mood than the beauty of the sky, against which the turrets and domes of the palace were etched in all their fantastic detail.

As usual her footsteps were echoed by those of her two guards, following tall and cloaked as she went in under the arcade, which was lit by wall lanterns that cast her hooded shadow against the wall.

She turned suddenly to face the guards, indicating with a gesture of her hand that she intended to enter the bey's quarters. She waited a moment to see if they would try to stop her, and when they made no attempt to do so, Lorne proceeded to open the arched door, momentarily at a disadvantage because the room was in darkness. As she stood hesitant, one of the guards strode past her and lit the lamps for her.

"Merci," she murmured, pushing the hood away from her face and displaying what she hoped was the pensive look of a girl who was pining for her lover.

She felt the dark Eastern eyes flick her lamplit hair, then, with an inclination of his turbaned head, the man joined his companion in the courtyard.

Lorne breathed a sigh of relief and glanced around her. She was rather surprised by the ambience of the room, which was obviously used as a lounge. Though the carpets were magnificently Oriental, the couches were in black hide, bereft of cushions. There were curios displayed in cabinets and shelves of books. A replica of the palace banner hung upon a wall, and beside it there was a damascened casque and a scimitar whose curving blade was inscribed with Arabic script. The hilt of the weapon was agleam with rubies and diamonds, as if symbolic of the tears and blood that the barbarous blade had probably caused.

It seemed a fitting ornament for a room in which Razul Kebîr took his ease. It seemed to fit the personality of a man whose act of treachery had brought her to this moment.

Out of curiosity she was drawn to the bookshelves and was amazed to find titles in a variety of languages, including Russian and Greek. She examined a couple of the English books and found they were on such subjects as military philosophy and the study of veterinary medicine.

Perhaps the most fascinating object in the room was an inlaid chess table beside one of the couches, on which stood, already in action, a set of warrior chessmen, superbly detailed.

What thoughts entered the mind of Razul Bey when he sat by himself in this room, smoking one of his dark-leafed cigarettes, his more amorous exploits held in reserve for when he visited the *serai*? The chessboard and the books suggested a man with a good mind, and Lorne didn't doubt his intelligence. She had seen for herself his look of culture, overlaid by the innate barbarism that had made it possible for him to abduct her, with a total disregard for the terror she suffered in the process.

Lorne felt a surge of temper and was reminded of why she was here. She noticed on his black wood desk a dagger with a lot of silverwork on the hilt, which he probably used as a letter opener. She picked it up and decided it was just what she needed for forcing a lock, and, carrying one of the lamps, she entered another of the silent rooms. This was a rather formal room, with a fountain at the center. The column of the fountain was in blue tile-work with raised patterns, and it played its cool soft music in the silence of the night, in the emptiness of a room, which Lorne decided was where the bey dined alone or with his male friends.

She discovered his bedroom through a doorway of fretted woodwork, that exquisite fretwork that allowed the air to filter into the Eastern houses during the day.

Lorne slowly glanced around her, seeing a low, wide couch draped in netting, which prevented insects from crawling over the occupant in the night. There was a bedside table, upon which a book held a leather marker. There were leather jacks with riding boots in place and, on a dressing stand, something that caught and held Lorne's attention. It was a face in a filigreed frame of silver, and walking carefully, like the intruder she was, Lorne went across the room and looked into the eyes of the woman pictured there.

It was Razul Kebîr's mother; Lorne was in no doubt of it. She didn't believe he was the type of man to keep in his bedroom the photograph of any other woman, and the face in the frame was that of a European, her hair in a woven chignon, wearing a silk dress with a rose on the shoulder.

She had been quietly, almost sadly beautiful, as if tragedy had marked from the beginning her marriage to Razul Bey's father. A marriage that had been doomed, with only the birth of their son to give it any durability.

Did he resemble her in any way? Lorne held the lamp so the light played over his mother's face, and she was startled when the eyes of a long-dead woman seemed to flicker with tiny points of amber. So that was why Razul Bey's eyes seemed at variance with the rest of his Eastern looks. Their color came from the woman who had borne him, the only outward sign that he wasn't as full-blooded a man of the East as he looked, especially in his Eastern robes.

Lorne lowered the lamp and turned away from the gaze of his mother, whose belongings she had come to disturb in her search for the jeweled fan. Lorne saw it all so vividly, the Frenchwoman falling unconscious to the sands, left there for dead among her scattered clothing, the body of her French husband beside her.

That had to be the chest, its paint work worn away by time, pushed against a wall of the bey's bedroom. Her fingers gripped the hilt of the knife she had brought into the room, and only a kind of desperation brought her to her knees in front of the chest. She edged the blade into the aperture between the lid and the bulk of the chest, thrusting at the lock with every atom of her desperate strength.

"Come on, come on..." she muttered, striving for the click that would release the lid. She began to think that it wouldn't happen, that the blade would break before the lock ever yielded.... When the click occurred, it seemed to fill the room, and Lorne took a hasty glance over her shoulder, as if it must have penetrated to the ears of the two men in the courtyard.

With a shiver of self-repulsion she dropped the knife, and for several moments she couldn't bring herself to raise the lid. It was like an act of sacrilege, but having gone this far, Lorne had to go all the way. It was a point of no return, and Lorne felt certain she would never forget the scent of old cedarwood and faded perfume that arose from the garments that lay folded away. With a tentative hand she touched a dress of layered organdy, whose whiteness had aged to ivory. There was a dragonfly-green dress, its winged sleeves carefully folded, a tea-rose silk and a blue linen with matching, pale blue stockings.

These dresses, apart from the photograph, were all that remained of Razul Bey's mother, and Lorne felt a rush of guilt, a sense of trespass that made her glance around the lamplit room, as if afraid of seeing a shadowy form, watching as she disturbed the garments in her search for the velvet fan case.

At last her fingers located the case, and she laid it aside without opening it. She knelt there, feeling the nervous beat of her heart. Though instinct warned her to close the chest and be gone, there was something here, something that held her immobile. *Déjà vu,* she thought. The feeling that had overswept her the first time she had found herself in the palace of the bey.

It was his mother, his very own mother, whose presence she could feel. The woman who had brought romantic dresses with her on a trip through the desert, unaware that the love and glamour would end in bloodshed.

Lorne's fingers stroked absently a fold of copper satin. It was a sad, fateful story, the young widow but a shell of her former self, a cloud over her mind and over her heart, even though she had wed in El Karah a man who cared for her. She must have loved the son she had borne him, but in the silences of the night had heard a Gallic voice calling to her from the lonely desert sands. Even her baby hadn't kept her from that reunion.

Lorne shivered from head to toe and was on the verge of closing the chest when she felt an acute sense of being observed. Though she feared the insubstantial, she just had to take a look—and she would have cried out, if her voice hadn't frozen in her throat. No shadowy form stood looking at her with accusing eyes. The tall, cloaked figure was that of the man she had believed to be miles away from El Karah.

"What a pleasant greeting." He spoke with heavy sarcasm. "The sight of the saintly Lorne, going through my possessions with all the skill of a practised thief. This, the vestal virgin who almost swoons when a man breathes upon her. This, the outraged girl who called me a libertine."

Lorne was close to swooning at that very moment. She stayed on her knees, too petrified to move as Razul Bey advanced toward her. She felt like a creature caught in a trap, and it flashed through her mind that the nuns were right when they said that a sin was always bound to find you out.

She felt herself shrinking as the bey loomed over her, the folds of his cloak falling apart to reveal breeches and boots that were dusty from a long ride.

Almost casually he began to beat off the sand with his braided riding whip, an action that was significant in itself. "Have you an explanation to offer me?"

When she remained silent, his eyes raked from her kneeling figure to the open chest, from the silver knife to the velvet case, lying adjacent on the carpet. When he leaned down to pick up the case, Lorne felt a stab of fear that was unlike her former reaction to him. Now he had the right to call her a thief, caught in the act of stealing a treasured memento of his mother.

As she watched him, wondering how to justify her actions, he flung off the splendid cloak of rich black cashmere and stood there in a kind of regal contemplation of her crouching figure. His feet in oxblood leather boots straddled the carpet runner, his breeches and tunic enhancing the power of his frame, his head robe bound by an *agal* of twisted black horsehair.

The stabbing brilliance of his gaze seemed to go right through Lorne. She was transfixed by his eyes, wishing with all her might that she was having a nightmare from which she would awaken—soon, before he carried out the threat that smoldered golden hot in the look he was running over her.

His eyes swept the disorder of her hair, caused by her struggle with the obstinate lock of the chest, then he glanced at the case in his hand. Suddenly he clicked it open and revealed the gemmed beauty of the fan that, on an evening in the desert, had sparkled in a woman's hand, while she sat with her husband under the huge clusters of stars. A woman unaware that her happiness was coming to an end.

"How dare you even touch this!" The words came with
the suddenness of a whiplash. "How dare you sneak into my
domain and tamper with my things? If I ever doubted that
you were akin to Lionel Desirée, then I have no more
doubts. He, too, was avaricious of what didn't belong to
him."

Lorne flinched, for the words seemed to strike her in a
physical way, and if she retaliated that his cousin, the princess, had promised her a horse in exchange for the fan, he
would be privy to plans she still meant to carry out—one
way or another. Somehow she'd get away from a man who
could make her feel so low.

Gathering the scattered forces of her courage, Lorne flung
back the hair from her brow. "Are you going to give me the
traditional seven strokes of the whip for my insubordina-
tion?" she asked with a bravado she didn't actually feel.

"I am strongly tempted." He glanced at the riding whip
in his left hand. "And yet I feel that seven kisses would
subdue you far more than a whipping."

At the look on her face that his words evoked, he gave a
low and grating laugh.

"You don't like the idea at all, do you, *ma fille*? *Non,* you
would prefer me to sting your skin with my whip, but your
punishment isn't going to be that easy, not when I find you
in the act of stealing from a chest that I know to have been
locked. Have you always been a thief?"

Lorne flushed vividly and scrambled to her feet. Her
knees were shaking, and never in her life had she felt such a
rush of mortification. "I—I'm not a thief," she blurted. "I
wasn't stealing the fan—"

"What a barefaced lie, young woman. The fan case was
concealed among the garments in the chest, which informs
me that you had a good search, that you were obviously
looking for an object of value. What was your motivation,
eh? Were you going to try and bribe one of my servants with
it? People who have served in this house for a long time.

People who know the history of the fan. People who would risk their very necks if they dared to accept such a bribe."

Once again his eyes swept her up and down. "You have less sense than a hinny, do you realize it? There are other artifacts in my apartment that would be far more acceptable—the knife, for instance, which I presume you used to force the lock."

She gazed at him in silence. Every portion of Razul Bey seemed menacing to her in those moments of stretched-out silence. His height, the way he was dressed, the sudden click of the fan case as he closed it.

"Has anyone told you about this fan?" he asked abruptly.

Lorne wildly debated with herself. She wondered if the Princess Jamaila had known that he was returning to the palace tonight. Even so, would he be likely to believe that his cousin had suggested she steal the fan?

Lorne searched his face, its every feature as detailed as the golden masks placed by the people of El Karah on the tombs of their kings. Though his eyes had taken their color from his mother, their expression and shape were Eastern. Tiger gold and slanting beneath dangerously black brows.

Lorne decided not to mention the Princess Jamaila. If she was jealous, then she might still be willing to help Lorne get away. It was a small ray of hope, which would be firmly stamped out if she told the bey how she happened to know about the fan.

"It looked valuable," she said. "That's the reason I took it out of the chest."

"And you were planning to use it as a bribe?"

"Yes."

"It must have come as quite a shock when I walked in on you?"

"I'd hardly risk being caught in your rooms if I had known you were about to walk in. I—I took a chance, and I got caught. You take chances, as well, Razul Bey. You took one in bringing me here in the first place, so why be surprised that I steal in order to buy my freedom?"

"Unhappily for you, *ma femme*, you took the one thing that would never buy you a horse—I assume it was a horse you were after and not a camel?"

"T-there's no need to be sarcastic," she rejoined. "At least you know that I wasn't stealing for the sake of it."

"Is it of importance to you, that I don't regard you as a thief?" He spoke almost lazily, yet the intentness of his gaze was impossible to evade. It was as if he suspected that she had not told him the whole story.

"I wouldn't want anyone to think me that low," she said.

"Not even a libertine and a seducer, eh? Not even I?"

"Not even you," she agreed. "I suppose you wouldn't do the generous thing and supply me with a horse?"

"Do you fondly imagine that Bar-Soudi would be so easy for you to find?" He spoke mockingly. "Even we of the East get lost in the desert, let alone a mere girl. And what would you do if another storm overtook you?"

"At least I wouldn't have to be afraid of falling into your hands, my Lord Razul."

"You might, young woman, fall into hands less clean than mine." His eyes narrowed until their golden steel seemed to be cutting into her. She backed away involuntarily from such a look, for menace had crept into the atmosphere of the room, and she knew she wasn't going to like what was going through his mind.

"I am the Lord Razul," he said, "and my powers of retribution are quite extensive. Would you like a taste of them?"

Her heart pounded, and she looked around wildly, as if for the flaming abyss that would save her from the bey's arms—if that was what he had in mind?

He laughed softly, a sound like silk and sand grains. "Fate is the only woman who keeps her secrets to herself.

Earthly women have eyes all too easy to read—no, *femme blonde*, I am not in an amorous mood right now.''

"What are you going to do?'' The words broke nervously from Lorne. "You know why I forced the lock of the chest—I've owned up, haven't I?''

"Have you?'' He glanced at the fan case, which was still gripped in his hand. "Aren't you curious about the fan? Don't you want to know to whom it belonged?''

"I—I assume it was a woman whom you loved.'' Lorne's sense of apprehension was in her voice.

"But such an assumption didn't stay your hand, did it?'' He spoke curtly. "In fact, I am surprised that you think me capable of loving anyone. Am I not heartless? Am I not a tyrant with a heart of stone?''

Before Lorne could find an answer to his question, his manservant appeared in the open doorway, carrying a tray of refreshments. The bey spoke to him in Arabic, and after Abdul had placed the tray on a coffee table, he glanced swiftly at Lorne, making her wonder what Razul Bey had said to him.

"Don't look so apprehensive.'' He calmly flung off his cloak and kicked shut the lid of the chest that Lorne had ransacked. "I have not told my servant to heat up the branding iron.''

He flung himself down on a divan and gestured at the coffeepot. "Pour me a cup, and don't shake it all over the carpet.''

Lorne felt like throwing it over him, and with compressed lips she poured the piping hot coffee from the swan-necked pot of glowing silverwork. She added brown sugar to the cup and handed it to the bey, sprawled at his ease on the divan. The braided whip, the silver knife and the fan case lay on the tabletop, and Lorne wondered again what he meant by retribution.

The look he gave her as he drank his coffee was less than benign. She saw in his eyes some devilish intention, but he

merely said, "Do help yourself to a biscuit. Abdul is bringing another cup so you can drink coffee with me."

Oh, was that all? Lorne wanted to believe it, but instinct
warned her that Razul Kebîr wasn't so easily mollified. "I'm
not at all hungry." She plucked restlessly at the cloak, which
was still around her shoulders. "May I go to my room? I'm
feeling tired."

"Worn out by your exertions, no doubt. No, you will stay
here until I am ready to dismiss you."

"Dismiss me?" she exclaimed. "I'm not a schoolgirl!"

"You have behaved like one—like a foolish child, caught
with her fingers in the jam cupboard."

"Are you planning to cane me?" Lorne stood rigidly in
front of him, chin held high even if her spirit was flagging.

He quirked a black eyebrow at her defiant stance. "I have
to admire your gall," he said. "But you have to be stopped
from doing yourself harm, and it is my intention to see that
you are stopped."

"A caning won't stop me," she retorted. "I'll crawl across
the desert if I have to."

"Doubtless." He held out his cup and saucer. "I would
like another coffee, for one gets thirsty riding in the desert."

With a mutinous look on her face, Lorne replenished his
cup. She added sugar with a look that implied that she
wished it was poison. "Merci." He smiled briefly, as if
reading her thoughts. "Do remove your cloak and relax,
petite, for it isn't yet bedtime."

Her heart skipped a beat, and with reluctant fingers she
unclasped her cloak and allowed it to slide from her shoulders, revealing her in a kaftan of deep silky blue, with a
collar and cuffs of the crusted embroidery, that was so
Eastern. Feeling far from relaxed, she sat down on one of
the big floor cushions, which were always scattered around
the rooms.

Abdul returned with a cup and saucer, and with a politely inscrutable face, he poured coffee into the cup, added cream and handed it to Lorne. She met his eyes for a moment and wondered if she only imagined a fleeting look of sympathy in them. Then he turned to the bey, who again spoke to him in Arabic, though Lorne was aware that Abdul spoke fluent French.

She sipped her coffee, which, as usual, was richly aromatic and had a delicious taste. Abdul departed, and once again Lorne had to endure the intimacy of being alone with Razul Bey in his bedroom.

"What a relentless man you are!" The words wouldn't be held back, no more than the half-pleading look that she flung across the room at him. "I know you're up to something—and that I'm not going to like it."

"For the present, enjoy your coffee." He took a long, almost black, cheroot from a humidor and lit the end. He puffed out smoke and allowed his turbaned head to rest against the cushioning of the divan. His very look of total relaxation made Lorne terribly aware of her own state of tension.

"You're the last man to be sitting in judgment on me!" she exclaimed. "I've picked up my disgraceful habits since you brought me here, do you realize that? I was a good girl—well, a fairly obedient one, and I wouldn't have dreamed of doing what I've done tonight. It would have seemed like inviting hell and brimstone."

He slowly raised an eyebrow and didn't take his eyes from her face. "Hellfire, eh? Haven't you invited it tonight?"

Lorne bit her lip until it hurt. Oh God, what was he going to do to her? All sorts of things filled her mind, especially with that net-shrouded bed in her line of vision. "You enjoy tormenting me," she accused.

Quite deliberately, he glanced toward the bed, and his smile curled around the cheroot he was smoking. "I was right, eh? Seven kisses of mine would be far more tortur-

ous for you than anything else I could think of in the way of
retribution."

"Retribution!" She leaned forward, her eyes flashing
deep blue beneath the wave of hair that fell half across her
brow. "Anyone would think I'd stolen the crown jewels of
El Karah to hear you talk. It's only a fan—"

"You had no right to touch it, not without my permission," he rapped. "You come sneaking into my apartments
when my back is turned and you rake over my mother's
clothing—"

He broke off, glowering through the strong smoke of his
cheroot. "Yes, my mother's clothing...my mother's jeweled
fan. Doubtless you noticed the European style of the dresses
in the chest?"

"Yes," Lorne breathed. "Yes, I noticed."

"And are you going to pretend not to know that she was
French, and brought to El Karah after being found half
dead in the desert?" It was Razul Bey's turn to lean in passionate tension toward Lorne. "Were I a fool, *ma femme*, I
would not be paramount chief of this region. You knew you
were stealing an object of very great value to me, and that
makes the offense all the more reprehensible. You knew,
didn't you?"

"Yes," Lorne admitted, her feelings seared by the contempt in his eyes.

"Who told you? Was it Kasha? She was my nurse, and
she knew my mother."

Lorne had to let him assume that Kasha had told her
about the Frenchwoman who had borne him. She was
clinging to a thread of hope where the Princess Jamaila was
concerned, for if the princess was infatuated by Razul Bey,
then it would be to her advantage to rid the *serai* of a rival.
Perhaps she hadn't known that the sheik was returning tonight to El Karah. Lorne couldn't be sure, for the simple
reason that she hadn't yet learned to read Eastern minds as
easily as they seemed to read the European mind.

They seemed to have a subtle intuition, which left Lorne feeling at a loss as she sat looking at the bey of Karah, who showed not a hint of his European blood, or did she glimpse it in his build? He was physically bigger than most Eastern men she had seen in Bar-Soudi, and though several of his guards were tall, they weren't quite so broad in the shoulder. Somehow his size made him tower over other people, and that would add to his luster as their leader.

"How much do you know of my mother's story?" he demanded.

"I—I know that she died while you were still a baby."

"From injuries received in the desert, from which she never fully recovered. Or—" he glanced at the ash that had built up on his cheroot, then he flicked it off "—did her heart never mend?"

A shiver ran through Lorne, for there was in his words that strain of fatalism that was so much a part of his culture. A thing happened because it was written in the sand. The will of Allah.

"My mother died when I was born," Lorne said quietly. "But you know that, of course. Lion told you, and it was true, even if you thought that he was inventing it in order to soften your attitude with regard to the plantation."

"Then we have something in common, don't we?" But his eyes didn't soften toward her; his features didn't relax their sternness. "Tell me, would you like it if I came in stealth to your bedroom and took a personal belonging of your mother's? Would you consider it an act to be lightly dismissed?"

She didn't consider it an act to be proud of, and his anger was understandable, but in return he had to understand that she'd use whatever means she could in order to regain her freedom. He had taken from her something of far more value than a jeweled fan, and she felt no inclination to hang her head in shame.

"There would be no need for your anger or my stealthy behavior if you did the honorable thing, Lord Razul. You could do it this instant. You could tell one of your men to saddle me a horse, and you could let him guide me to Bar-Soudi. Why do you keep me here, when you know how much I hate you for it?"

She flung out a hand toward the chest with its forced lock. "Haven't I proved how much I want to go? I knew how angry you would be—"

"But you believed you would be up and away before I returned, eh? When I walked in on you, *ma femme*, you almost leapt out of your skin."

His eyes ran over her, but still with a hard look in them. "Such smooth white skin, so without a flaw, lending you such a deceptive look of innocence. What is the English saying? As if butter wouldn't melt in your mouth."

"You abducted me," she flung back at him, "and that's a far worse crime than the one I've committed. Of course, you wouldn't see it that way. Your fairness, tolerance and mercy are reserved for your own people—and you are wholly one of them, aren't you, my Lord Razul? There is very little of your mother in you."

"Which is to say that you consider the French more civilized?" He snapped his fingers, as if self-justification was something he didn't even think about. *"C'est la vie."*

"Whatever happiness I had at L'Oasis is in fragments, and you're the cause of it." Her eyes blazed with accusation. "And you don't give a jot, do you?"

He stubbed his cheroot in a brass ashtray and he didn't take his eyes from her face, eyes as mesmeric as those of a tiger stalking its prey. "It was the sirocco that blasted L'Oasis, and it was a stroke that took your grandfather out of your life. You would like to believe that I am a deep-dyed villain, but the truth is that each one of us is cursed with original sin. There are no saints on this earth, though there are heroes. There are no angels, except in our mythology. We are all driven by the earthly nature of what we are.''

"In that case, Lord Razul, you shouldn't be treating me as if I've broken some eleventh commandment of your very own. I'm flesh and blood. I have feelings, and they aren't always angelic. You—you're going to do something, aren't you?''

"I am going to ensure, *mon amie*, that what happened to my mother in the desert will not happen to you.''

What on earth did he mean? Lorne felt a tightening of her skin, even as Abdul appeared in the doorway and directed into the room a man in tarboosh and robe, who gave the customary obeisance and greeting. His sharp dark eyes and hawkish nose gave him a predatory look, and Lorne could feel herself going rigid as he was followed in by a pair of assistants who carried a brazier, which they handled with gloved hands. She stared at the men, and a hand slowly lifted to her throat, where her pulse beat against her fingers like the wings of a trapped bird.

As the brazier was carried to the center of the room, Razul Bey rose to his feet and approached Lorne. "This is a goldsmith, *mon amie*, not the local inquisitor. He is not about to apply a branding iron to your white skin.''

Lorne sat immobilized by the scene in front of her, by the flames that leaped and flung their heat toward her, casting brazen shadows over the faces so they took on a sinister look. "What is he going to do?'' She flung a look of appeal at the bey, whose face gave nothing away as he stationed himself behind her.

"You will not make a fuss.'' His hands descended upon her shoulders. "Sit still, and it will all be over in minutes.''

"W-what is going on?'' Her voice had risen, as if forced into a higher pitch by the alarm that gripped her by the throat.

The goldsmith stared into her eyes, then slowly drew a leather pouch from his pocket. He opened it and took out something that gleamed bright gold against the darkness of his hands.

He came toward Lorne, and as she tensed in the grip of the bey, he pressed his fingers into her bones. *"Douce-ment,"* he murmured, as if to a filly that was on the verge of taking fright. *"Doucement."*

"You damned devil!"

"Be still, unless you want to be burned." He increased pressure against her shoulder bones, and Lorne watched in disbelief as the goldsmith encircled her right ankle with the band of gold, then calmly riveted the anklet with a slim iron that had been heated red-hot in the brazier.

It was happening—she could smell the metal and feel the heat against her ankle. Then the operation was over, and the goldsmith had climbed to his feet. He bowed to the bey, and he and his assistants withdrew from the room, taking with them the hot glow of the brazier, which left in the air its tang of charcoal.

"It's rather attractive." Razul Bey had let go of her, and she sat rigid as he kneeled in front of her and examined the anklet. "It has been inscribed, as you can see. The words are in Arabic—"

"You're full of sadistic tricks—" Lorne glowered at him, the feel of his fingers an affront, the outrage of the riveted anklet almost more than she could believe.

"You have no idea of sadism," he rejoined. "If you take it into your head to run away, and you fall into the hands of nomads, they will see from this inscription that you belong to me, in which case, they will neither harm you, nor sell you. They will return you to me with your virtue unimpaired."

"You're despicable—"

"No, I am merely observant of the rules of the desert, which deceives with its beauty in the same way as a woman deceives. Look what your lips are capable of saying, and they are such tempting lips."

He was on his feet in one agile movement, and he had brought Lorne up against him, locking her to him until there wasn't a part of his body she wasn't aware of, a fierce aliveness that she tried distractedly to avoid. But, with a strength she could never match, he drove down upon her lips, her head pillowed upon the muscles of his arm as he forced open her lips until she was overpowered by his kiss. It was the most intimate of sensations, and tiny shocks went up her body.

"Six more kisses to go," he breathed.

Arched over his arm and helpless, Lorne could only fight him with words. "Isn't it enough—that you've made a slave girl of me?"

"If only your nature matched your temper, *mon ange*. Your upbringing among the nuns must have made you so—reluctant."

"I—I'm merely immune from your devastating charm," she retorted.

He smiled slowly, his dark lashes making shadows around his amber-colored eyes. Then, abruptly, he stood her upright and gave her backside a stinging slap. "What I do, I do for your own good."

"Thanks—for nothing." Her buttock was tingling, and she stood there and tried to look as dignified as the situation would allow. He confronted her as if expecting her to lash out at him. "Now may I go to bed, my lord?" she asked, in a cool, mock-sweet voice.

Quite deliberately he cocked an eye at his commodious bed, and Lorne backed hastily away, feeling the touch of gold against her ankle.

"Come," he said, "I will walk you to the *serai*. Tomorrow you might like to sort out some things from my mother's chest—not the fan, my dear. That isn't for any other little girl who fancies it."

Lorne gave him a startled look and received a sardonic one in return. "Are you being serious?" she asked. "You were furious with me for touching your mother's dresses."

He gave a shrug. "I am aware that you feel uneasy in Eastern clothing, and though my mother's dresses might be *démodée*, I don't think that will concern you very much."

Lorne didn't know what to say, and they walked silently to the *serai*, beneath the ramparts of his palace and the rooftop flutter of the tribal banner. Lorne could feel her golden shackle as she walked beside Razul Bey, and she wanted to refuse his offer of the dresses, with their Paris labels and the lingering perfume in their folds.

The courtyard lanterns cast his formidable shadow along the flagstones, and Lorne decided that prudence was the better part of valor.

"All right," she murmured. "If you don't mind?"

She felt his sideways glance, skimming her figure in the cloak that she had resumed wearing. Her nerves gave a leap—then settled down when he paused in the entrance of the *seria*.

"I will bid you good-night." His fingers gripped her chin, and he raised her face so he could look down into her eyes. "I shall warn my servants to ignore any requests of yours that are unrelated to your welfare within my palace. Do I make myself clear?"

"Transparently," she murmured.

"It had better be so." Suddenly his other arm was inside her cloak, and he pulled her hard and fast against him. He lowered his head and laid a hard kiss upon her lips—a kiss of threat rather than passion.

"Go to your bed." He swung away from her, striding across the courtyard, tall and dominant in the light that fell here and there from the lanterns, pallid bands of ghostly shadow that broke the darkness, revealing among the stone arcades the vigilant stillness of the palace guards.

CHAPTER EIGHT

LORNE'S FINGERS GRIPPED the stonework where she stood, feeling the deep impressions of intricate carving. Then she turned quickly and hurried into the *serai*, trying to blot from her memory the daggering fire and danger in the embrace of Razul Kebîr.

How dared he do these things to her, as if her very reluctance was a spur that drove him on! The anklet was there to remind her constantly of him, bearing in letters of gold the outrageous statement that she was his property, to be returned to his custody if she went astray.

She stared down at the glistening anklet, and once again she seemed to hear his whispered words, and she touched herself where he had landed a far from gentle slap.

"What I do, I do for your own good," he had said.

Well, if he thought she was going to tolerate a slave band around her ankle, like some ringed pigeon, then he was mistaken. She called imperatively for Kasha, who came hurrying into the room. "What is it, *lel-lah*? What's wrong?"

"This!" Lorne extended her leg, with its offending attachment. "This is what's wrong!"

Kasha scrutinized the anklet, then gave Lorne a curious look. "My Lord Razul has put it there?"

"Of course he has—he's had the thing riveted on, and I won't stand for it! Fetch me a nail file, I'll try and saw it off—"

"You cannot do that," Kasha exclaimed. "He would be furious with you."

"I'm furious with him! Is there a file in that box of cosmetics?" Impatient with her maid, Lorne stormed across the room to the inlaid cabinet and flung open drawers. She found the box and spilled out the cosmetics with a careless disregard for the cloud of face powder that fell to the carpet. "Here we are!" She was delighted, for the file was a sturdy one with an ivory handle. Raising her foot on a floor cushion she set to work, sawing away at the rivet that held the anklet in place.

"It's of gold," Kasha said, shaking her head as she watched Lorne. "It won't yield, *lel-lah*, if you try all night to make it do so."

Lorne looked at Kasha through a tumbling wing of hair. "He has no right to do this to me—"

"It is our custom." Kasha spoke in a consoling voice. "It isn't as if my Lord Razul has had an iron shackle placed around your ankle."

"That's what it feels like." Lorne flung aside the useless nail file. Kasha was right, of course. The anklet was solid gold, and she was wasting her time trying to get free of it. The anklet was riveted on for as long as Razul Bey desired, and she belatedly wished that she had told him what he could do with his mother's old-fashioned dresses.

She pushed a hand through her hair, but it was a gesture that pushed away the thought. Even as she had handled the lovely fabrics, she had felt an affinity with the woman who had worn them long ago. A woman who, like herself, had fallen into the hands of a man foreign to her. A woman who had lost her husband, just as Lorne had lost her grandfather. The pair of them in a situation of a strange similarity.

"You knew his mother, didn't you, Kasha?"

"Yes, I knew the Lady Lily."

"So that was her name?" Lorne reflected on the lovely
face in the ornate silver frame. "She was elegant, wasn't she,
like the lily?"

"Yes, she was like a pale cool flower, with huge eyes and
a long slim neck, which bore a burden of golden hair."

"Fair hair!" Lorne's hands gripped each other. "Like
mine?"

"Not exactly. Hers was a deeper gold with shadings of
copper. You are a perfect blonde, *lel-lah*, and you are
younger than she was when they brought her in from the
desert. She had been hurt there, her husband killed." Kasha looked troubled. "I don't know if I should be telling you
about her. My Lord Razul is very reserved about her."

"I've seen her photograph in his rooms," Lorne said
quietly. "The strange thing is—he has offered me the use of
her dresses."

Kasha looked astonished. "For years they have been
locked away, ever since she died when he was ten months
old. His father ordered it so, and he never took another wife
after his loss of her. I remember her funeral so well, the long
line of camels carrying the mourners into the desert, where
she was laid to rest. It was her wish, and my lord's father
carried it out."

"So she never forgot her first husband? He was the one
she loved the best?" That funeral cortege wended its way
through Lorne's mind.

"Love?" Kasha spread her hands, as if in her lifetime she
had seen enough to make her wonder if love was worth the
pain. "It is written in the Koran, in life you can only have
one great love."

"One great love," Lorne murmured, slowly dropping her
cloak from her shoulders. "Razul Bey probably knows that
his mother never truly loved his father—I wonder, is that
why I'm here, because of some grudge he can't forget?"

"You are here, *Inshallah*." As she spoke, Kasha took
charge of the bedtime ritual.

Lorne submitted to the ritual but not the remark. "I'm here because of the will of a devil—you all know it, so why pretend otherwise?"

Kasha retained an inscrutable look as she helped Lorne to undress. In bed at last, and alone, Lorne lay and reviewed the events of the day and the way they had culminated in Razul Bey's unexpected return.

It was true, she had almost leaped out of her skin when she had turned to see him looking at her from the doorway. She wondered how long he had stood there watching her, for he had an almost tigerlike way of walking, silent and dangerous. Lorne pressed her face into her pillow and lay in a curve, as if protecting herself from her thoughts of him.

Thoughts that dwelt on details she longed to forget . . . with possessive arms he had held her to him, and his warm lips had left their impression on hers. Even yet she could feel his kiss, piercing her memory and invading the inner sanctum of herself.

Dear God, if she didn't get away soon from him, he would force more than his kisses on her. Her toes curled into the undersheet of the bed, for her mind wouldn't back away from an image of herself, flung over his arm with such devastating ease. Added to his physical strength was his innate attitude toward women. Their function was to divert, amuse and provide the sons to carry on his so important name.

Lorne's thoughts turned to his mother, who had clung on to her love for the Frenchman she had lost in the desert. Lorne's fingernails dug into the fine linen of her pillow. What was Razul Bey's real purpose in bringing her to this place, where the Lady Lily had never recovered the will to live with any man other than the one she had lost?

If Lorne hadn't been so personally involved, then she would have found the story of the bey's mother an intriguing one. Instead, she lay in the grip of speculation, wondering if he was driven by some emotion he couldn't control.

Lorne lay on the verge of sleep, wondering if Razul Bey was making her pay for the loss he had suffered, when long ago the Lady Lily had been carried back into the desert, a long line of mourners following her on camelback.

The idea seemed fantastic, and yet Lorne couldn't get it out of her head. She fell asleep and dreamed of camels wending their way across the dunes, until they were quite out of sight and she was on her own in the desert. Alone and afraid, she started to run, but the camels and their riders were gone and their flowing cloaks had stopped making patterns in the air.

She cried out for someone to tell her why Razul Bey kept her with him in El Karah. But in her dream no one heard her.

She awoke at a later time than usual, and when she pushed aside the filmy bed drapes and sat up, her eyes fell upon the arabesqued chest, which she had last seen in Razul Bey's bedroom. Her heart skipped a beat. So he had meant her to explore the contents and perhaps find something she could wear. He had seemed confident that she wouldn't mind the old-fashioned style of the garments, and this was true. Lorne hadn't a lot of vanity, nor had she been reared to the idea that looking démodé was the ultra aim in life.

Throwing aside the bedclothes, she ran on bare feet to the chest, and this time, when she kneeled in front of its faded decoration, she could open the lid without that awful feeling of trespass. Everything had been neatly refolded, and Lorne wondered if she could bring herself to sort them over.

With a touch of reverence she stroked the apricot silk of a blouse with a *broderie* collar. Had the Lady Lily worn these things around the palace, preferring them to the Eastern clothes of a bey's wife? Lorne drew a fold of silk to her nose, and because the garments had been under lock and key for such a long time, there was still a fragrance clinging to them. Lorne decided that it wasn't an Eastern scent. It was more delicate, hinting at Paris and a stylish woman who had loved a man so much she had followed him into the desert, taking with her the clothes she would have worn to smart dinners on terraces above the boulevards.

It was so sad, Lorne reflected. Two people in love who were never to see again the city that was so different from the exotic beauty and danger of the desert. Its strange beguilement had called to them, the call that Lorne herself had answered when Lionel Desirée had sent for her.

Lorne was kneeling there in her night toga, lost in thought, when she felt another kind of signal. It went up and down her spine like a touch, and she had no need to turn around. She knew that the bey was observing her.

"*Bonjour, mon amie.* I see that you are busy with your *cadeau*?"

"My present?" she murmured, still without looking at him. She was too conscious of her near state of undress, that if she stood up, the diaphanous fabric of her night toga would reveal more than she wished to show him.

Oh yes, she was aware that he was acquainted with her figure, but each time the bey looked at her, it was as if he looked at her for the first time. No matter what occurred between them, it was swept away when their eyes met. The danger in the man was never sublimated to any kind of gentleness, and she was startled that the word should occur to her. She didn't ask for it. She didn't expect it, not from the man who had confronted her in the desolation of L'Oasis without a word of compassion.

"Yes, I'm giving you the contents of the chest," he said. "I believe Kasha has a sewing machine, so she'll be able to assist you in altering the hemlines."

"I—I don't think—it doesn't seem right," Lorne faltered.

"What doesn't seem right?" In a stride he was beside her. "Look at me and explain yourself."

With something of an effort she looked up at him, her still uncombed hair tumbling about her face and neck. "They've been locked away a long time—it seems such a pity to disturb them."

"You had no such compunction last night," he reminded her.

Her eyes wavered from his. "There's no need to throw that in my face. I've explained—"

"Have you?" His voice held a fine edge of irony. "My apartments were the last place you'd visit, unless someone told you what you might find in the chest. Don't take me for a fool, *mon amie*."

"As if anyone could?" Lorne pushed the hair from her brow, an action she regretted, when his eyes followed the movement and what it revealed beneath her night toga. She had a wild wanting-to-hide kind of feeling, like that of a trapped creature when a predator came too close.

"So you are throwing my gift back in my face?" There was a sardonic look in his eyes, as from his formidable height he regarded her, making Lorne instantly aware that her posture was somehow slavish, there at his booted knees.

"I—don't know if it's right," she said again. "The fabrics are lovely, but—"

"You have reservations because the woman who last wore them was my mother?"

"No—"

"Non?" Something flashed in his eyes. "That is how it seems."

"It isn't that." Lorne shook her head. "I was brought up to believe that the soul lives on after a person dies, and after seeing your mother's photo and hearing about her from Kasha, I feel as if—as if I know how she felt."

The bey stood silent, as if sorting out in his mind the clumsy meaning in what Lorne said. "You mean how she felt about being the wife of my father, a man she loved less than she loved the Frenchman who lay buried in the desert?''

Lorne inclined her head, but what she really meant was that it was strange and alien to be a European woman in the hands of a man to whom women were creatures to be adorned, faces to be admired, bodies to be enjoyed. She couldn't see beyond that bred-in-the-bone attitude. She couldn't believe that men of the East ever thought of women as companions, for they seemed to enjoy the company of other men when it came to discussing aspects of life unrelated to the physical. They surely held the view that women had featherbeds for brains. She could see it in his eyes— couldn't she?

And then he said the same thing as Kasha. "According to the Koran, *mon amie,* you can have in life only one great love, and it would seem that my mother's great love was not my father but the young Frenchman." And as he spoke, Razul Bey held Lorne's gaze with his, with those compelling amber eyes.

Then he reached for her and drew her to her feet, and the sudden feel of his hands sent those memorable shock waves up and down her lightly clad body. The moment had a fatalistic feel about it, and there was something sensually evocative in the way he held her.

The complexity of her feelings held her in another kind of grip. Her knees felt tremulous, and she couldn't make a sound. She could only gaze at him in a kind of speechless expectation. And as he drew her nearer to him, she felt such a current of awareness that it caught her by the throat. All she could see was the lean jawline, those distinctive eyes, that entire air of pride that was purely Eastern and rooted in the very sands.

Through the veils of her lashes she watched him and waited, looking into those brooding desert eyes.

"There is no reason why you should repudiate the dresses," he said. "The fabrics are fine, as you said, and

Kasha has skillful fingers. She will help you to make them suitable for you."

"Then if you don't truly mind..."

"I don't mind, truly." He said it with a faint hint of mockery. "How young you are, still with the teachings of the convent clinging to you."

"Don't you believe that the soul lingers on?" she asked.

"Men of the East are taught to believe that women have no souls."

"No wonder men of the East are arrogant." Lorne tried to dispel the vulnerable feeling his closeness evoked. She stood straight, between his hands, and tried to be unaware of herself. "May I ask what we have in place of souls, Razul Bey?"

His lips curled slowly into a smile, and he slid his eyes over her. "If you don't know, *mon ange*, then you are in grave danger."

Lorne caught her breath. "W-what is that supposed to mean?"

"I think you know; otherwise I am losing my touch."

His touch...fingertips warm and vibrant against her body through the yellow rose fabric. With an effort she stood rigid, trying not to be affected by him.

"I never doubted your skill in dealing with women," she fenced. "I expect you started young."

A brief laugh broke from him. "Do you imagine that the boys of your country are any different? Let me put it like this, *mon enfant*, there are always girls who are willing, and there are always those who are romantic. Who would have believed that Lionel Desirée would have such a one for a granddaughter?"

"My mother was a romantic," Lorne said, and a tremor shook her lips. "I expect I take after her, just as you take after your father."

He raised a black eyebrow, tauntingly. "Would you like me a little better if I looked and behaved more like a Frenchman?"

"Perhaps," she said grudgingly.

"I see." His hands deliberately pressed her closer to him. "I am the bey of Karah, and you will have to endure my barbarity in place of kisses on the hand."

"I—I don't have to endure anything—"

"Don't you?" He lowered his head until she could feel the warmth of his breath on her face. His look and his breathing were almost a narcotic, which made her eyelids feel as if they wanted to close. She fought the compulsion, for she had read in books that women closed their eyes when they succumbed to a man, and she didn't want Razul Bey to get such a preposterous idea in his head.

"You think me the soul of barbarity, eh?"

"I don't think education has turned you into an intellectual," she agreed. "I know you read books in a variety of languages, and I don't doubt your ability to train an army or cure a sick animal, but at heart, Razul Bey, you're like some overlord of olden days, when even the kings had kings."

"Ahh..." He slowly released his breath, as if he had been listening intently to her. "And what are you, at heart? Perhaps my slave girl in that other life—that life of resurrection believed in by my people?"

"We wouldn't have met—"

"Would we not?"

"My roots are in Gaul."

"And mine in the desert, eh?"

"Oh yes."

"At this point in time we are well and truly face-to-face." He gazed down at her, the amber of his eyes flickering with thoughts she could no more read than the Arabic language. "We are just a man and a girl, and I think I shall lay you on the bed and prove to you that the body is the master of us all."

Words that made Lorne's heart turn over. "Don't—please—"

"The words don't go together," he taunted, swinging her up in his arms with supreme ease. "But you and I—that is another matter."

Lorne kicked her legs in an effort to escape him. "Your consuming ego—let go of me!"

"I shall consume you, if you don't stop hurling such words at me." The breath shuddered through Lorne as he dropped her to the bed, and she tried to scramble free of him as he joined her on the bed, boots and all—and intentions she couldn't doubt as he started to fondle her through the fine-spun fabric that barely concealed her from his black-lashed eyes, agleam with golden fire.

"Y-you're a devil without any humility—" She shuddered from her neck to her heels as he drew his hand slowly down her body.

"You," he murmured, "are no angel. Stop thinking of your nun's school. You weren't made to be a nun." His hand caressed the slender curve of her hip, and his fingers trailed lower to her thigh, which he stroked through the toga, which seemed to add a sensuality to the movements of his lean, warm brown fingers.

Lorne wanted him to stop—didn't she? She wanted to despise every bone in his body—didn't she?

She felt a tumult of emotions, and they were all on the surface of her skin, and her skin was reacting to his touch in a way she couldn't seem to control. A breathless gasp escaped her, for his hand lay warm and firm against the most private portion of her body, that part of the body that the nuns had been so strict about, so that it had to be covered even in the bath.

Lorne wanted to protest, but the words wouldn't come. She wanted to thrash about so he would remove his hand, but instead she lay there as he stroked her, until sensations of innermost bliss were sending flutters and tremors up over the smooth skin of her stomach. Her heart pounded and her lips parted, and she felt as if she were floating away from herself.

How far would he have gone, if Kasha hadn't walked into the bedroom? "Oh, I do apologize, my lord!"

Lorne heard the words dimly, then the bey's lazy reply. "Yes, I know I must keep an appointment. What a pity!"

He raised himself on his elbow, shielding Lorne with his body as he studied her face in its tousled frame of blond hair. "Duty calls, little one, and I have to leave you. What a deprivation!"

"I . . . I'm glad . . ." But her voice was blurred, and her hands wanted to reach up and clutch his head. . . . She wanted him down upon her, close and hard, with the world forgotten.

Their eyes dueled, and he seemed to know all about the conflict that was going on inside her head. He smiled, a wicked glimmering of amber eyes, shaded by those dense black lashes that she had felt against her skin.

He bent his head and took her lips in a slow-moving kiss. "We leave off now, *mon ange*, but tonight we can start again."

But common sense was rushing in to dispel the madness. She was coming to herself, and with the fierceness of self-hate, she thrust her hands against his shoulders and pushed him away from her. That he moved was due only to his will to move. Otherwise, she could never have shifted him.

He stood up, leaving her lying there in the disarray he had caused, and for seconds more he enjoyed her with his eyes.

"Don't—look at me like that." She rolled over and curled herself into a ball, and with a throaty laugh he left the room. She heard his deep voice as he said something to Kasha. Her cheeks burned to have been seen with him on the bed, so obviously in the throes of being caressed by his expert hands...those hands that had pleasured the other women in his life.

How many were there? Lorne had never dared to ask Kasha if he came to the *serai* to sleep with any of them. She had shut herself off from knowing, and it didn't strike her as strange that only the Princess Jamaila came into her apartment. She was aware that she was kept in seclusion, the foreign girl with the pale-colored hair, whom the bathing attendants laughed at because she absolutely refused to be plucked and painted until she resembled a porcelain doll.

She sat up, cuddling her arms around her body. "I'm me," she reassured herself, but it was still disturbing that she became such a stranger to herself whenever Razul Bey willed it. His touch seemed to bring out some hidden part of her, the part that her school days had repressed.

No wonder the nuns had been so strict with the girls; they had known, without explaining, the wiles and wants of the male sex. Oh Lord, how shocked they'd be if they could see Razul Bey, with his arrogantly graceful body and his eyes that could reach into a girl's mind and read her most secret thoughts.

They'd think her fit for burning in the fires of retribution if they knew what that desert devil did to her when he touched her. She laid her face on her updrawn knees. "Tonight," he had said. "Tonight we can start again...."

With a gasp Lorne scrambled off the bed and ran through the bead curtain into the bathing room. Kasha had drawn her bath, and it bubbled and fragrantly steamed. Lorne leaped in and went through a ritual of cleansing that certainly left her body in a pristine state. The same couldn't be said for her mind, which was filled with provocative images in which Razul Bey was hero and villain.

When she finally climbed out of the sunken bath, Kasha wrapped her in a large towel, almost protectively. Their eyes met, and Lorne gave a wistful kind of smile.

"You mustn't mind, *lel-lah*, that you are pleasing to my Lord Razul. He's a man of many duties, and it is pleasant for him to relax with you."

"I suppose it doesn't matter if I'm pleased or not?" Lorne sat on a stool while her hair was dried.

Kasha gave her a slightly reproving look. "You seemed very relaxed, *lel-lah*."

Lorne flushed to her earlobes. "He makes me feel things I don't want to feel, Kasha. He doesn't love me—he just makes use of me."

Her maid shook her head slightly.

"Well, he does," Lorne insisted. "Oh, I don't want to be one of *them*."

This time Kasha looked puzzled.

"One of his *women*." Lorne infused a note of venom into her voice. "Something for him to enjoy—like *couscous!*"

"Then what does the *lel-lah* want?"

"You know what I want."

"Are you quite certain?" Kasha stroked a brush through Lorne's hair, bringing it back to its fair luster after its energetic rubbing.

"Of course I'm certain. Do you imagine that I'm like the others—mad about him? You know full well that he does exactly what he wants to do, regardless of anyone's feelings."

"Then you didn't enjoy his caresses?"

Lorne was about to shake her head when innate honesty made her compromise with a shrug. "The bey has been with women since heaven knows when—practice makes perfect!"

Kasha caught her breath, as if unused to such candor where the bey was concerned. "You are wrong in what you say, *lel-lah*."

"I was there—you saw me with him, didn't you?"

"I mean . . ." Kasha hesitated, trained as she was in discretion where the secrets of the *serai* were concerned. "You spoke of his other women, but there are none."

"I don't believe you." Lorne had convinced herself that, in secluded apartments like her own, Razul Bey had women of all shapes and colors, awaiting his attentions with bated breath.

"I speak the truth, *lel-lah.*"

Lorne gazed up at her maid with astounded eyes. "But men in his position, don't they have heaps of women?"

"Some," Kasha admitted, "but Razul Bey has never been of that kind. When he has enjoyed the diversion of a woman, she has been with him as you are. He is not a voluptuary, but like other men he likes to have a lady friend. This is natural, it is not, *lel-lah*?"

"So I'm the latest in a string of lady friends?" Lorne looked cynical. "Part of the *hors-d'oeuvres* until he takes a wife, I presume?"

Kasha followed Lorne into the bedroom, where she helped the girl slip into a silky kaftan. Lorne gestured toward the painted chest, still with its lid thrown back so the glimmer of fabrics could be seen. "His high and mighty lordship informs me that you have a sewing machine, Kasha. With lordly generosity he has offered me the use of his mother's dresses, which presumably he has never done before with one of his lady friends?"

Her maid's silence answered her unspoken query. His other diversions had been women of the East, so there had been no problem about what they preferred to wear. The diaphanous floating garments would have suited them.

Frowning slightly, Lorne walked over to the chest, but the moment she caught a whiff of the delicate perfume, which the years had trapped like a memory, her mood altered. She beckoned to her maid. "Shall we look through them, Kasha?"

They spent the remainder of the morning sorting out suitable dresses that Kasha could alter and hem on her machine, an old-fashioned Singer that still functioned well. By lunchtime a sleeveless, cream-colored dress was ready for Lorne to wear. There were pale silk stockings to go with it and a pair of sandals, which were quite a good fit.

Lorne whirled round in front of the mirror, looking and feeling like the girl she had been at L'Oasis. "This is more like it," she enthused. "I was getting fed up with looking like a vamp, even if his lordship prefers the type."

When they met at lunch, he merely quirked an eyebrow. "I see you found something to your satisfaction," he remarked.

"Yes." Lorne found it difficult to look at him, for the memories of their last encounter were still potent, still too vividly recalled. "Did your meeting go well?"

"Excellently."

There was a glimmer of amusement in his eyes, which Lorne decided to ignore. "I found a pair of riding breeches in your mother's chest. I—I'd love to go riding, Lord Razul."

"Doubtless." He threw a peeled almond into his mouth. "I'm well acquainted with your wish to get into the saddle."

She gave him a reproachful look. "It isn't fair of you to keep me boxed up—like a candy bar y-you take nibbles at when you feel inclined."

"I don't intend to keep you boxed up for very much longer."

Her eyes flew wide and blue to his face. "You mean—?"

But before she could get out the words, he gave a brief, rather edged laugh. "I mean that I am arranging a trip into the desert."

"And I—I'm to go along?"

"Assuredly."

"Oh—" she felt a stab of impatience "—don't be so inscrutable."

"We are known for it," he drawled. "Do you fancy such a trip?"

"Yes," she breathed. "I should love to get away from this place."

"You say it in such a heartfelt way, *mon amie*. Is the *serai* so distasteful to you?"

"You know the answer to your question, Razul Bey."

"Doubtless." He shrugged his shoulders, wide and always threatening beneath his tunic, which was open at the throat to reveal the supple brown skin of his body.

Lorne's thoughts dwelt on the women who at various times had shared his life. Who had probably kissed him with eagerness, only too happy to find themselves in the arms of a man whose virile looks were undeniable. Then, in time, he would have grown disinterested in their eager kisses and their willing bodies, and each one would have been paid off, perhaps with diamonds or emeralds. He was rich, powerful, dynamic—and he was ruthless.

A shiver ran like a ghostly touch over Lorne's skin. Would she...could she escape him without becoming just another woman who passed through his life, like a thread of silk through the eye of a needle, sewing a memory he quickly forgot? Or would he remember her as the one who had dared to fight and argue with him? The one who refused to submit to his charisma.

Oh yes, he was charismatic; there was no doubt of it. He was the chosen leader of his people, and according to the Princess Jamaila, he was biding his time until his virgin bride was of an age to come to his bed.

In the meantime... Lorne tilted her chin to a chilly angle. She was here, and he had found it amusing and diverting to lay her on a bed and run his strong, expert hands over her body, which was every bit as virginal as that of the girl he would marry.

Through his lashes he was looking at her, studying the chill that had fallen over her features. "What are you thinking, *mon amie*? What gives you that look of a figure carved in ice?"

"Thoughts," she rejoined.

"Thoughts not for sharing?"

She was partially tempted to express what was going through her mind, but in that instant the servants entered with their meal, whose aroma, when the lids were removed, was too appetizing to be resisted. She ate in silence, and when coffee was served, she took her cup and sat on a kneeling cushion, at a distance from him. As he drank his coffee he watched her.

"Yes," he said at last, "I was right to suggest that you have some of *maman's* dresses altered for you. That dress suits your style of looks."

"Yes," she agreed. "I don't enjoy looking like an Eastern vamp."

"You think of yourself as a vamp, eh?"

"In keeping with what you think of me, my lord, though admittedly an inept one."

"Ineptness can always be remedied."

"In your expert hands?"

"None other." Suddenly his mouth hardened. "You seem to have a touch of the blues."

"My very profound apologies, Lord Razul. I don't doubt that you usually leave your ladies in a state of rapture."

"My ladies?" He took a cigar, flicked a flame at it until it drew, then let out a puff of aromatic smoke.

"The lady friends who come and go. I'm one of those, aren't I, though probably the only one who was unwilling. I expect all the others were hopeful that you'd stay intrigued by their charms."

He lounged with his feet up on the couch, and that his cigar was very much to his satisfaction was written all over him. He looked the very picture of relaxation.

"Your imagination is quite lurid, *mon amie*, no doubt the result of being in a chaste environment during your formative years. Yes, I have had my flings, but had I indulged in them to the extent that you imagine, then I would never have got around to my most important duty, that of regional bey."

He drew on his cigar and slowly exhaled the smoke. "I think you wish to start a fight with me. Why, I ask myself. Because I spoke of wanting you tonight?"

Lorne quivered at the words. "I—I don't care to be wanted like an object."

"How do you care to be wanted?" He sat studying the tapestry in which the girl had been stung by a scorpion placed in her basket of fruit.

"As a human being, that is, if I were interested in that sort of activity."

"But you aren't interested, eh?" He laughed to himself. "You very much amuse me, *mon ange*. Do you imagine that when I held you in my arms and touched you with my hand, I didn't feel your response to my touch? A denial would be a lie on your lips, so don't bother to make it."

"You think yourself so smart, don't you, Lord Razul? So above a woman in every way. So much the master of your destiny, with little consideration for the women you fancy and then throw aside. Haven't you loved any of them?"

"Love is an evocative word," he replied. "What do you mean by it?"

"Caring for someone, cherishing that person—oh, I don't pretend to know about it."

"But you have thought about it, eh?"

"Doesn't everybody?"

"There are exceptions."

"You, for instance, my lord?"

"It does occur to me that love could be more trouble than it's worth. It didn't make a happy man of my father."

"But those were sad circumstances." Lorne gazed at the intricate patterning of the carpet at her feet. She was clad in sandals that once upon a time the bey's mother had worn, perhaps with this very dress. Lorne jumped suddenly to her feet, as if a hand had brushed against her. "Oh, what am I to do?"

Razul Bey stared at her, then abruptly he stubbed his cigar and came to where Lorne was standing, her hands clenching the skirt of the cream-colored dress. "You are a bundle of nerves." His hands took hold of hers, clasping them so she couldn't snatch free. *"Doucement, mon ange, doucement."*

He spoke in a deep, persuasive tone of voice, but Lorne felt driven to pull as far away from him as she possibly could. She wouldn't be seduced by him—by his voice, his touch and those eyes that were as beckoning as the desert.

"I'm not a horse that needs gentling!" She almost wrenched her wrist bones as she fought his hold on her. "If you don't let me go, then I'll scream rape. I'll yell it at the pitch of my lungs!"

His eyes narrowed at the word, then he let go of her so abruptly that she stumbled and almost fell. He made a kind of gesture, as if plucking some unspoken words out of the air, and moments later the bead curtain was rattling and swaying behind his departure from the room.

Lorne nursed her left wrist, which was reddening from his grip. No, his lordship didn't like that word, did he? It was what he had on his mind, but he didn't like hearing it spoken aloud. It had to be wrapped up like an Eastern parable, convoluted and almost obscured, like the designs of the palace architecture.

Damn him for a devil! But even as she thought it, the tears were smarting hot in her eyes. The bead curtain swam and trembled in front of her, while the room filled up with a silence that blended with the scent of cigar smoke, lingering in the air until Lorne felt it would stifle her.

She ran from the room and made for the garden of turtles, the only creatures she felt she could trust in this palace
of the bey.

CHAPTER NINE

THE ORDER CAME UNEXPECTEDLY, just when Lorne had told herself that, in keeping out of her way, Razul Bey was doing exactly what she wanted him to do. Kasha was to pack for her. The trip into the desert that he had spoken about was imminent.

"I'm not bowing to his every command." Lorne refused to budge from the divan in order, at his command, to go to the stables to choose a horse. "He thinks he has only to raise an eyebrow to have everyone running their feet off. Don't dare to pack a thing, Kasha. I've no intention of going with him."

"But I have every intention of taking you." He strode into the room, his jaw as adamant as rock. "You will do as I say, Kasha, not as this little *bint* dictates. Up on your feet, *mon amie*, this instant!"

Lorne sat mutinous, then gave an audible gasp when he picked her up with effortless ease and dropped her to her feet. "Come with me, and close your mouth before you say something we shall both regret."

"You—bully." Struggle as she might, Lorne was led firmly from the *serai* into the hot sunlight of the courtyard. The furious blue look she flung at him was offset by the cool blue linen of the dress that Kasha had cleverly altered. Its color and its slim, cool lines suited Lorne, and with it she wore linen sandals, which felt the heat of the flagstones as she was led to the palace stables.

The cool stone corridor of stalls was occupied by Arabian horses, their heads sleek and handsome, their huge soft eyes belying the iron of their mouths and their stamina.

"I thought you dreamed constantly of owning a horse." Razul Bey looked her over in her blue dress, against which the light gold of her hair was both casual and arresting. "I am about to present you with one."

"How magnanimous of you, my lord. What do I give you in return, a kiss on the hand?" Despite her defiance, Lorne felt a stir of excitement. To own a horse was her second most fervent wish, and she was well aware that Razul Bey's horses were of the finest stock.

"Don't go leaping to the conclusion that you'll be allowed to run away on it." His eyes glinted, but not with amusement, as he escorted her along the line of stalls. "Now take your choice, *mon amie*. Show me how much you know about horseflesh."

"Each one is a beauty—" Then she caught her breath, for in that instant she had seen the horse of her dreams, a sorrel with a thick upstanding mane and a chasing look in the eyes. She paused and fearlessly touched the glossy, deepchestnut coat. "You really mean it, Lord Razul? I may choose any horse of my fancy?"

"I never go back on my word, even though you choose Oseille, who has a habit of throwing out of the saddle anyone who climbs into it."

"He won't throw me," she said confidently, not backing away as the spirited horse started to chew the front of her dress. She firmly pushed his head aside, determined to have him, determined to show how able she was in the saddle.

Razul Bey beckoned one of the stable boys and spoke to him in Arabic. The boy opened the stall and led out the chestnut, who tossed his mane and got a wicked glint in its eyes as the saddle was flung across his back. The saddle was of scarlet leather, hung with silver-worked stirrups. Lorne was eager to show off her ability as a horsewoman, but she obviously couldn't do so in sandals and a dress.

"I need boots," she said, and though in her sandals she was standing dangerously close to the restless horse, she didn't move away.

Razul Bey took her by the wrist and pulled her away. He said something to the stable boy, who returned to the room where the saddles were hung and emerged with a pair of boots whose kidskin surfaces were quite unscuffed. They looked brand-new, and Lorne gave the bey an enquiring look.

"From Kasha I learned your foot size," he said. "These boots have been handmade for you."

"I see." Lorne hated to feel grateful for anything he gave her. "I had riding boots when I came here, but they were taken away from me."

"Of stiff English leather." He dismissed them with a flick of his hand. "You will find your new ones far more supple and easy to wear. Take them."

She did so, with a mumbled thank-you.

"I shall wait here while you go and change." He seemed disinterested in whether or not she was pleased with his gifts.

She ran off, clutching the boots to her. When she reached her room, it took her no more than a few minutes to tug off her dress and replace it with a silk shirt, found among his mother's belongings, and the odd wraparound trousers that stood in for riding breeches. As she stamped into the kidskin boots, Lorne had a painful memory of herself in her bedroom at L'Oasis. It was loyalty to Lion that had kept her from leaving the plantation when Sadik had urged her to do so. She couldn't abandon him, even though he lay dead and unaware that she chose to stay in the storm-racked house.

Loyalty and gratitude had been her downfall, and they were emotions she didn't want to feel ever again.

She dashed back to the stables, where Razul Bey's silvery-gray stallion had been saddled, and the gateway of the stables flung open to the desert. Razul Bey dropped his cheroot to the ground and placed his heel on it. The look he gave Lorne was a fully comprehensive one.

"Here you are." He offered her a riding crop, which Lorne accepted. Then, eagerly, she approached Oseille and took hold of his bridle, watched by the stablehands as she placed her foot in the stirrup and swung her leg over the chestnut's back. She felt him tauten, and as she sat down in the saddle she gripped the reins and spoke to him in dulcet, soothing English tones. "Now behave yourself, you red devil. Don't make me look an idiot by throwing me on my backside in front of His Lordship."

Oseille pricked up his ears, as if noticing the difference between Lorne's voice and that of the boys who attended to him. His hooves beat an iron warning on the flagstones, he tossed his tail and glanced sideways at the stranger in his saddle.

Lorne pushed her feet firmly into the stirrups, aware at once that the supple kidskin made this easier than if she had been wearing her stiff English boots, with their tendency to resist the Arab stirrups. She sensed that Oseille was going up on his hind legs a second before he did so, and she clung on firmly rather than desperately.

"You aren't going to topple me, Oseille." And, biting her lip, she brought the crop down on his gleaming body. He quivered, as if amazed that a slip of a girl should treat him so. He had obviously taken it for granted that he was going to unseat her without any bother at all.

"Behave yourself," she ordered. "Stop being a brat."

Somewhere beyond her concentration on the horse, Lorne heard an amused growl of a laugh. Her chin tilted, her hands tightened on the leather reins. What was Razul Bey hoping for? That she would prove incapable of handling one of his precious Arabians? She cast a quick look at him as he bounded into the saddle of his own mount, who reared, settled, then reared again, straining at the bit to be off into the desert.

"Come! Ride!" The words were flung like a challenge at Lorne, and she dug in her heels and signaled Oseille into a canter. It was now or never. The horse would either obey her command or do his utmost to throw her off his back.

He stood very still, and leaning toward his handsome head, Lorne cajoled him. "Be friends with me, big boy. I desperately need someone I can trust, and you are such a handsome devil, Oseille. Make up to me for losing Firefly. Be a darling."

He scraped a flagstone with an iron-shod hoof, flicked his tail, shook his bridle until it rattled and jangled. Lorne felt his proud resistance to her, a resistance she understood, for wasn't she in the same position where the bey of Karah was concerned? Her fingers gripped the riding crop, but she didn't use it again. Suddenly Oseille flung up his head, as if getting a whiff of the desert beyond the gateway.

There it lay, limitless and tawny, ridged with sun-burned dunes, the figures of Razul Bey and his mount etched against the gold. Then Oseille plunged in the wake of the silvery-gray stallion, and Lorne felt the warm air of the desert brush like a well-remembered touch upon her face.

She caught her breath as the bounding strides of the chestnut carried her away from the palace. She flung a look behind her and saw the turrets and domes receding in the sunlit air, dissolving like the mirage she wished they were.

The chestnut surged alongside the stallion, and Lorne suspected that Razul Bey was holding his mount in restraint until she became accustomed to Oseille. Anyway, she couldn't hope to match the bey when it came to horsemanship, and there was no denying his superb skill, bred in his bones along with his other Eastern instincts.

His cloak billowed, and he was a picturesque figure as he sat astride the powerful gray, and wordlessly they galloped along, the sand flying upward from the hooves of the horses. Salukis, lean hunting dogs of the desert, sped along in the tracks of the horses, and the air was tangy with a mixture of scents, driven in over the desert from the mountains and the sea, miles beyond the high bastion of sunstruck, gleaming rock that created a skyline almost menacing.

The exhilaration of the gallop shone in Lorne's eyes when they finally rested the horses beneath a clump of palm trees. Razul Bey dismounted, but for a breathless moment Lorne remained in the saddle of Oseille. *Take a chance!* The words whispered through her mind. She had got the feel of her mount. She felt herself to be in control of him, and it was the answer to her prayer, to have her hands on the reins of a horse with such speed and stamina.

"Forget it!" The words crisped through the air. "I would catch up with you, and even if I didn't, you would lose yourself. *Mon amie*, though the desert might look deserted to you, there are nomads who make it their constant home. As I've told you before, their hands are less well washed than mine... less polite in every way."

Lorne sat, tense in the scarlet saddle, and her gaze fused with his. There was a burning power in the look he was giving her, an awareness of her feelings, a stillness that threatened far more than any movement of his figure and face.

Lorne's fingers gripped the crop that he had given her, and her fingers could feel the indentation of Arabic script in the silver handle.

"Dismount and let the horse take a breather."

She shrugged and did as she was told. It was foolish to argue with him here in the desert, and when the Salukis came bounding around her, she found relief from his eyes in making a fuss of the dogs. They knew her, for they were always in and out of the *serai*, either chasing each other or being chased out by Kasha, who scolded Lorne for allowing them on the couches. Lorne had the English love of dogs, but she knew that, primarily, these agile hounds were used by the bey and his men for hunting game.

He had flung his cloak over one shoulder, and it trailed his oxblood boots as he came toward Lorne. "You are a fine horsewoman," he informed her. "Desirée taught you well."

"Lion also taught me how to shoot," she said in a cool voice. "I think had I lived with him all my life, instead of being a pupil at a school run by nuns, I would have shot you that morning you came to L'Oasis. My trouble, Razul Bey, is that I was taught to be too trusting of other people and their intentions."

He stroked the head of one of the Salukis, and the animal nuzzled him with a whine of pleasure. "If I spring my intentions upon you, it is my way. Our sojourn in the desert has already begun. I gave orders for the servants to follow on with the tents and the camping equipment, and they should catch up with us in about half an hour."

"You truly are the limit," Lorne exclaimed. "Taking it for granted that I'd want to camp in the desert at a moment's notice."

His eyes narrowed, then he gave a mocking inclination of his head, bound in a black-and-gold turban that emphasized the bronzed, clear-cut authority of his features. "Perhaps, as I am older than you, *mon amie*, and a man of the desert, I discern your secret desires before they occur to you." He swept his braided whip in a gesture that took in their tawny surroundings, the undulating ridges of sand that were like golden waves stretching to the limits of the imagination. Overhead, the sky was so blue it was breathtaking, and there, against that azure canvas, the dark wings of desert hawks were etched, as they hovered, then dived on an unsuspecting pigeon among the rocks of a sun-dried *wadi*.

"Tell me to my face that the desert doesn't intrigue you," the bey ordered. "I would bet that, from the moment you came East, you felt the magnetism and the mystery. Every aspect of it would be so different from what you had experienced behind the gothic walls of a convent school. The colors and aromas would be like a honey wine that you were unable to resist. Tell me, *ma femme*, that this wasn't so.''

Lorne's fingers clenched on her riding crop. Oh yes, Razul Bey excelled at reading her mind. To him, she was a transparent page out of life's book, and with experienced eyes and instincts he deciphered her thoughts . . . her feelings . . . even desires that seemed to lurk in some undiscovered part of herself.

''You must admit that you drag me along.'' She spoke with a cool haughtiness. ''I get told, not consulted.''

''Do you fondly imagine that I would consult a *bint* like you about my plans?'' His lip curled with amusement. ''What a lot you have to learn about me and my ways. One of the reasons why I arranged this trip into the desert. Here we shall learn about each other, for this is the garden of all wisdom, the playground of the gods.''

''Not to mention the serpent,'' Lorne interposed, standing there in the shadow of the palms, daring his eyes, slim and straight in her white breeches, corn silk shirt and knee boots. She felt to the core the stabbing brilliance of his eyes, and she strove not to show the alarm that his words had evoked in her.

''I relish the danger and delights of the desert.'' He breathed in through tempered nostrils the *mélange* of aromas, his cloak thrown dashingly over his shoulder. ''I wish to share them with you.''

His words had a curious effect upon Lorne, an unexpected effect that she was quick to conceal by turning her head so she was looking away from him, across those infinite spaces, which time had left untouched.

''The desert at night is one of the most wondrous places on earth,'' he murmured. ''You have never been deep in its heart at night, when the stars overhead are so clustered together that they turn the sands to ivory. You have never eaten food prepared over a fire of blazing camel thorn. You have never slept in a tent of black hides, on a mattress of sheepskins—but tonight you will.''

Again that quivering deep inside Lorne... again a reaction to him that made her knees feel boneless. She leaned against a palm tree and tried to look cool and unconcerned, as if the innate meaning in his words had left her unaffected.

"Time does not exist in the desert." He stood, as if absorbing its splendor into the pores of his skin, his amber eyes agleam. "A footstep in the sand is erased by a breath of air. The passions of a thousand years are still the passions of tonight. Each dawn in the desert is unearthly and still, with no sign of the squalor that man creates when he has to live without this kind of breathing space."

Razul Bey took a deep breath. "I would live out my life here if that were possible, but it suffices if I can steal away and spend a short time in the desert."

He wheeled toward Lorne, his very cloak making a statement. "*Mon amie*, you are the only woman I ever brought on one of these sojourns."

Lorne gazed at him, not knowing what to say in answer to him. The desert was enthralling, and she feared her response to it.... It was as if she responded to the bey himself. A retort wouldn't leap to her lips; her mind wouldn't supply her with a barbed reply. She felt defenseless, even as he reached swiftly for her and swung her against him.

Lurid images swept her mind, then his whip cracked sharply, and something fell from the trunk of the palm tree were she had been leaning. She gazed downward at the scorpion he had just killed, and when she realized how near it had crept to her, she shuddered from head to toe. It had a cruel and stinging look even as it lay dead at her feet.

"They climb the trunks of palm trees." His breath fanned Lorne's skin and she shivered with a different feeling. "Are you about to swoon?"

"No!" She attempted to pull away from him, but his arm tightened around her, and she felt the pressure of his muscles, insistent and firm as he lowered his head until his mouth was but a breath from her own.

"I—I'm expected to thank you, I suppose?" There was a catch in her voice, and she turned her face quickly aside, so his lips met her ear instead of her mouth.

"When a man goes to the trouble of saving a girl's neck, he expects some recompense." There was a hint of mockery in his voice. "This is the desert, *mon amie*, with all its beauties and its dangers. Here it no longer matters that you are a Desirée and I am Razul Bey. We are two people who flared like tinder and spark from the moment our eyes met. Look at me." With a firm hand he made her do so, holding her by the nape of her neck as he studied her face, naked of any artifice in the frame of muslin, which bound her head. He scanned her features with sun-narrowed eyes, as if searching for the reason why they stood so close and yet were so far removed in understanding each other.

There was no sign of tenderness in his gaze, no suspicion of love, yet suddenly the desert was oblivion for Lorne, wiped out by the force of his lips on hers.

It was rather like the storm that had swept over L'Oasis, savagely out of control, frightening in its intensity...then suddenly as still as death. He turned away from her, and the reason was the jingle of camel bells moments before the long-necked animals and their riders came into view, a sight so Eastern against the tawny canvas of the sands.

Lorne was instructed to remount. "We have some distance to ride before we reach the place where our *douar* will be set up. I wanted you to get used to your horse.... Had you not done so, then you would have ridden there on my saddlebow."

Lorne stepped into her mount's stirrup, but she was still shaky from the kiss she had been forced to share. To her dismay her clumsiness made the horse jib, and suddenly she found herself asprawl in the sand. Razul Bey gazed down at her with a mocking expression. "Have your legs gone to jelly?" he taunted.

Lorne leaped to her feet, giving him a glare as she grabbed her mount's bridle. It added to her sense of outrage that his men laughed at her, and gritting her teeth, she swung into Oseille's saddle, jabbed with her stirrup and gave him his head. He dashed forward, and she lay low in the saddle, relishing the rush of air that cleared her mind of that kiss beneath the palm trees.

His kiss was ravishment enough without allowing herself to think of his intentions, now that she was with him in the golden wilderness of the desert, which he spoke of as timeless...the garden of the gods, where the passions of the ages were but the passions of tonight.

She was riding as swiftly from her thoughts as from the bey himself, for she didn't have to look behind to know that he was chasing her on his stallion. It could have been the ride of her life—indeed it was exhilarating...breathtaking. They thundered along in the blazing sun, over the ridges of rough-pelted sand, past gaunt sandstone rocks that were red-gold in the sunlight.

An ageless kingdom. The place of destiny. It is written, it is fate... No, she wouldn't subscribe to such a belief, nor submit to it.

She had been forced into this situation, and all that desert devil wanted was to make her bow down to him. Then he'd be satisfied; then he might let her go, uncaring of what he had made of her.

When his stallion surged alongside Oseille, the look that Lorne flung at him was stony blue. He was more picturesque than any man had the right to be, his cloak flying away from his shoulders, his face barbarously striking beneath the black-and-gold turban. There was an artistic side to Lorne, which betrayed her when she saw this man on horseback. He was like an incarnation of old, pagan days, and there was no denying his incomparable verve, the way he rode his powerful horse with a deceptive ease. The gray was a full stallion, the only kind of horse a tribal chief would ride, and Razul Bey rode him superbly.

So superbly that Lorne knew there was no getting away from him. He paced his gray so they rode in unison, and in a while the sun was no longer streaming over the sands like gold-shot mercury. It began slowly to turn to a great vermilion ball, and every imaginable color began to creep into the sky.

The desert beneath this flow of color was beautiful beyond words. Lorne filled her eyes with *la beauté du desert*, whose spell had fallen over her grandfather all his life, whose drama and enticement had led a young French couple into its dangerous heart, where they had loved and lost each other.

Lorne had a curious feeling that Razul Bey was taking her to where his mother had been found, and she felt the tumultuous beat of her heart as a group of trees and boulders loomed ahead of them, pillars of desert rock that had been sculptured by the winds into a primitive kind of temple. She glanced sideways and Razul's profile was as if cast in bronze by the declining sun. Untamed desert . . . untamed man, she thought, whose dash of French blood couldn't be discerned in his looks or his behavior.

Beneath that vermilion sunset, glorious and fierce, they reached their camping ground among the towering rocks, masses of shrub mimosa and tall Barbary fig-cactus.

The laden camels bristled their harelips as they were coaxed to the sands, which had turned to a mysterious shade of purple. Lorne slid from the saddle, feeling a shiver of afterexcitement and the sense of chill that followed the decline of the sun.

Thankfully the fires of camel thorn and tamarisk were soon alight, their flames leaping skyward around the long shovels on which coffee beans had been laid to roast.

Swift and skillful hands soon had the tents erected, the *grande tente* of the bey being the most commodious. It was pitched in the shadows, beneath the gaunt pillars of rock, its hide walls hung inside with carpets that kept out the night cold. There was a veiled-off area, screened by camel covers in deep, rich colors. The copper oil lamps were alight, and coffeepot and cups stood in readiness on a silver table placed in front of the couch of sheepskins.

Lorne stood tense in the flap opening, watching the servants as they prepared supper. The aroma of the roasting beans drifted on the dusky air, along with that of *couscous* in big iron pots. She felt stirred by the ineffable beauty of the starlit sky. To see such a sky was to believe in heaven... but it was a heaven disturbed by a tall, cloaked figure in the firelight, who came to where she stood after his task of seeing to their horses.

In pulling off her muslin turban, Lorne had left her hair in disarray, and before she could retreat, he had stroked a hand over its fairness. "Silvery ash and gold," he said, in those low, disturbing tones.

Lorne stood mute, and the crackling of the camp fires seemed over-loud to her, their sparks shooting high in the air as a shovel of beans was withdrawn.

"We are going to enjoy the tent life for a while," he told her. "The tent, to the desert dweller, is a pavilion of rest, set out on a terrace of gold. Come, let us go inside. Abdul will be bringing coffee, then, afterward, you may take a bath."

"A bath?" she exclaimed, looking up at him in wide-eyed surprise. "Here, in the middle of the desert?"

He drew her firmly inside the lamplit tent, where the hanging carpets gave the walls a mellow, comfortable look. He glanced around appreciatively, then he gestured at the section that was curtained off by the camel covers. "Behind there you will find a bath made of camel leather, and water will be fetched in camel-leather buckets from the well, which is mine, sunk deep among the rocks. As I once told you, a water well is of inestimable value to a man of the desert.''

"Will you build anew on the ground where L'Oasis stood?" she asked with a touch of constraint.

"I haven't yet thought about it," he replied. "Well, what do you think of our tent?"

Our tent! The words sent a thrill of alarm through Lorne, and she could no longer doubt that he meant to sleep in here. It would induce into their relationship an intimacy she could hardly avoid, and she had a wild urge to dash outside the tent.

Even as she felt the urge, he untied her cloak and removed it from her shoulders. "Go to the couch and rest yourself, *mon amie*. We have had a long ride, and you have had an Arabian horse to deal with, one bred from stock that traces its origins far back into the history of my family. You like Oseille?"

"How could I do otherwise?" If only to avoid his closeness, Lorne went to the couch and sank down on it. This came as a relief, for her legs had started to quake from the moment he implied that here in this tent they were going to live together.

"I give you the horse." He removed his own cloak and stood before her in black trousers with tapering legs that hugged the calf. His tunic was open at the throat and bound round his body by an embossed leather belt. He unhooked the stirrups from his knee boots of supple leather, and all the time Lorne was intensely aware of his tigerish grace and power. Every move he made was compelling, and here she was, in his *douar* in the dusky desert.

"Oseille is yours," he added, "but not if you are going to ride off on him, God knows where."

"Why should you care?" She pushed the abundant hair back from her eyes. "Are you any different from the nomads who attacked your mother? Was it here, Lord Razul, that she was found half-conscious?"

"Nearby," he admitted. He leaned down to a table and took a thin, dark cigarette from a box with a running gazelle painted on its lid. He flicked his lighter and watched Lorne through the flame. "Does it trouble you, *mon chou*? Are you afraid of ghosts?"

"Are you?" she retaliated. "They are your ghosts, not mine. They are your memories that won't be still in the night. Is that why I've been brought here? To detract you from your memories?"

"I was but an infant when my lady mother died." He stood smoking, with something threatening in his stance. "I have no memories of her. I have only seen her face in a photograph."

"You were ten months old," Lorne reminded him. "Even at that early age a child is aware of love and caring, then suddenly she wasn't around anymore to care for you. That precious link was broken, and in your infant's mind you couldn't understand why her special touch, her special way of talking to you, her special kind of caring were gone—gone for always."

Lorne was surprised by her own eloquence, but she felt compelled to go on. "Ever afterward, Lord Razul, you were afraid to open your heart to anyone, in case the person stayed only for a while, and then left you feeling bereft."

The bluish cigarette smoke circled his head, its strong aroma drifting to Lorne, whose eyes were trapped in his gaze. She could have counted her heartbeats in the silence that hung between them. Then he gave a dismissive shrug of his shoulders. "It's a romantic theory, *mon amie*, but as it happens I was never bereft of affection in my infancy. My father gave me all the attention he could afford from his duties, and I never lacked for caring. He never took advantage of Muslim law, which permits a man to have four wives so I was his only child. I was his son, and our people have a special kind of feeling for a boy child."

In that instant the flap of the tent was swept aside, and Abdul entered, bowing discreetly to both of them as he filled the silver coffeepot from a larger pot, filling the tent with the aromatic smell of the beverage. "The *lel-lah* will pour for me," Razul Bey said to him in French.

Abdul nodded and glanced around to see that everything was in order. "The water for bathing is being prepared, my lord," he said. "Dinner should be ready in one hour."

"Excellent." The bey smiled, and Lorne noticed a look on Abdul's face that startled her. The men who served Razul Kebîr were attached to him in a way she had never noticed at L'Oasis, between Lion and his staff. She remembered how they had run away when the storm winds began to howl around the plantation house, showing no sign of the loyalty that Abdul showed toward Razul Bey. No matter what the danger to themselves, she had the feeling that his men would stand by him, and something told her that it wasn't fear of his power that made them loyal to him.

A sigh escaped her as she leaned to the coffee table and filled their cups with the fragrant brew. When she raised her head, he was coming to the couch. When she handed him his cup and saucer, he was lounging at his ease, looking at her. "I begin to think that nothing I do to please you will ever please you," he said, stirring his coffee.

"This trip into the desert?" She allowed her hair to screen her face as she stirred her own cup. "You only please yourself, Lord Razul. How could you do otherwise, a man of your arrogance?"

"My arrogance," he murmured. "How little you know of men, and yet you must have witnessed in your own grandfather the will to bend life to his own purposes. How do you think this world was made? How do you imagine it's sustained? Man isn't all that different from a tiger, but things go wrong when he forgets to be a proud and wary animal."

"You don't forget it for a moment, do you, my lord?" Lorne held her cup between her hands and sipped the dark, soothing coffee. "Doesn't it ever worry you that the Princess Jamaila's brother might attempt to depose you?"

"I ensure that his wariness of me is greater than his ambition," the bey replied. "He has his entourage, those who support him for their own benefit, but I hold a greater sway over the tribe. I am eminent leader because I care about my people."

"And because you're so sure of yourself," Lorne exclaimed. "Is there never a moment when you feel unsure, like normal people?"

His gaze slid quickly over her face. "I am not made of stone, no more than you are." He touched her arm through the silk of her shirt. "*Très sensuelle*, and the color suits you."

"It belonged to your mother." She eyed him curiously as she spoke, for it seemed a stony gesture on his part, to allow her the use of the Lady Lily's wardrobe.

His fingers slid down to her wrist, where the cuffs of the silk shirt were linked by gold studs. "You mustn't expect of people that they be saints, *mon amie*. We are all at the mercy of our own quirks of behavior. Had you wanted the security of a cloistered life, then you would not have traveled to the East. You would have stayed where you were, but you felt the call of the desert. Deny it. Deny it to my face."

"I don't," she said. "But I didn't dream that when I came to the East I would fall into the hands of a—bandit like you."

"A bandit?" He seemed amused by the word, but there was indication of some other feeling in the way his fingers tightened on her wrist, so that the stud pressed against her wrist bone.

"What am I expected to call you?" she challenged.

His eyes dwelt on her lips, and she realized that he was impelling her toward him. "No—" she said, the word dying to a gasp as he pulled her across his lap and bent his head to hers. It was achieved so quickly, so forcibly, that Lorne was helpless in his arms, his lips on hers before she could say another word.

With a slow deliberation, he kissed her mouth, dwelling on it as if it were a fruit for his delectation. Even as Lorne felt a furious urge to batter him until he let go of her, a strange lassitude overcame the urge, and she found herself assailed by sensations so tingling that she could hardly bear to accept them in rigid stillness. Her toes curled as the lips of Razul Bey wandered warm and searching around her neck, then began a slow and teasing journey down inside the opening of her shirt.

Her fingers clenched against his back, where the muscles could be felt through his tunic. And as if he took this for a signal, his mouth pushed aside the silken barricade of her shirt. Lorne gasped as he kissed her breasts as he had kissed her lips, deliberately, with a persistence that brought her almost to the pitch of crying out—against him, and against herself for feeling as if she wanted his lips all over her.

"Don't—" The word came out stifled and breathless, as if it had burst the bonds of her inner conflict.

"Don't ever stop?" he queried, and his amber eyes looked directly into hers, as if he knew very well that he had broken through her emotional barrier and made her feel a desire of the body that overpowered her mind.

"Stop using brute strength on me—you know I can't fight it."

"Perhaps it is something else you can't fight." His eyes kindled with a deep-down smile. "Why fight me, when surrender feels so much more pleasurable?"

"I—I'll never give in to you—"

"Does that mean," he drawled, "that I shall have to take what you refuse to give?"

"But you said—" Lorne broke off, color suffusing her face as his eyes roamed over her, amused and just a shade calculating.

"You and I have said a lot of things to each other." He quirked an eyebrow. "Won't you be a little more explicit?"

"You must have been lying to me—"

"Lying?" Menace crept into his gaze.

"When you denied—when you said that rape wasn't what you had on your mind."

"I never have lied to you, believe me or not." As he spoke he ran his lips in a tantalizing way over her white skin. "Don't confuse the violence of rape with the way I treat you, *mon amour*. If I were hell-bent on having you I would have achieved my purpose the first night you were at El Karah. There was no one to stop me, least of all yourself. Do you imagine that a rapist sits and converses with his victim? Do you really think that I am in any way related to a mindless thug, set on causing pain and humiliation?"

Lorne's eyes were fixed upon his face, and it was impossible to see in him that kind of beastliness. But what she saw made her bite her lip. "You're trying to seduce me, aren't you? You aren't concerned about my pride and self-respect, but you'll expect the girl you marry to be pure as snow on the peaks."

The words hung between them, then he pushed Lorne from his lap and rose to his feet, always intimidating when he stood over her. With a shiver she jerked into place the shirt he had disturbed with his seductive lips.

"You are right, of course." His mouth had hardened. "Every man wants an innocent bride and I am no exception. I shall have her, make no mistake about it."

"I am just the *hors d'oeuvres*, is that it?" Lorne tossed her hair and tried to look as if she felt nothing but disdain. But she knew that a secret part of herself had been unlocked, as if he had found the key to the romanticism in her nature.

"I shall leave you to prepare yourself for our supper *à deux*." His amber eyes seemed quite aware of what Lorne was fighting—this insidious attraction between them that shook her defenses so they were in danger of toppling and leaving her quite at his mercy.

"Don't be afraid of desire," he said softly. "It's far more natural than chastity, and with those eyes of yours, you were never meant to be a stranger to passion."

"You can keep your passion," she said stormily. "Save it for your bride. I understand she's being kept in *purdah* until you're ready to say the word."

"With whom have you been discussing my wedding plans?" he queried.

"Your cousin, the Princess Jamaila. She couldn't wait to tell me about the girl who has been set aside for you."

"And are you jealous?" he taunted.

"Jealous?" She tilted her chin at the very idea. "Your vanity is equal to your arrogance, Lord Razul. You think every woman is in love with you.... You'll have to drag me to your bed!"

"Will I?" His lips curled into a smile. "There are many types of women in this world, and there are certainly those who give their all for luxury and ease."

"I'm not that sort." Her blue eyes blazed into his.

"Upon that point we agree. Tent life in the desert should appeal to you, *mon amie*."

"Yes, if I didn't have to tolerate your company."

"My company isn't so abhorrent to you. Shall I prove it to you?"

Lorne scrambled away from his touch, and he gave a laugh and bowed himself out of the tent, leaving her alone in a silence that made the encampment sounds beyond the carpet-hung walls an alien accompaniment to her thoughts. She listened to the activity and the language she couldn't understand, apart from a few everyday words. She heard the

jingle of camel bells as the animals munched their supper,
and caught the sound of a flute being played.

It was a wailing Eastern tune that drifted to her ears, en-
compassing all the strangeness of the people among whom
she found herself. Suddenly, she was startled as a hand
pushed aside the flap of the tent. It was Abdul and a boy,
both of them carrying buckets of steaming water.

Lorne followed them into the veiled area of the large tent,
where the camel leather bath had been set up. All the comforts of home, she told herself, and caught the boy giving
her an inquisitive look. She was the *kadin* of his bey. She
was the woman whom the master had brought along for his
enjoyment, casual as the hunting and hawking that would
take place during this vacation he had arranged.

Several more buckets of water were brought in, until the
leather tub was filled. Then she was left on her own, with the
camel covers drawn so she could bathe in privacy, using the
olive-oil soap, which Kasha had not forgotten to pack. It felt
good to soak in the tub after a long ride in the saddle, and
though her limbs were soon eased, the same couldn't be said
for her feelings.

It was as if Razul Bey's features had been branded on her
mind. As if his kisses had been branded on her mouth. Even
as she bathed, she relived the silken heat and ardency of his
embrace and tried to scrub away the feeling with the sponge.
She punished her skin, but still his touch had dominance
over her senses...senses that had lain dormant until he had
forcibly disturbed them.

Damn him for a devil! She flung the sponge, and water
splashed all over the place. She scrambled out of the tub and
wrapped herself in a big towel, recalling her school days and
the shifts she and the other girls had to wear when they
bathed. Always the basic lesson had been that the flesh was
weak and willing and must be subdued to a determined will.

All very well for the nuns, cloistered as they were behind
ivy-hung walls that kept them safe from men. Lorne was

miles removed from that coolly contained world of prayers and discipline. She was deep in the desert, with a man who lived by the rules of his own land, his own culture, where a woman was concerned.

A man whose striking face was haunting her, as was the tenor of his voice and the awareness of his touch.

His kissing had a maddening effect on her resolve. Desire! Love! Even as Lorne scoffed at them, she knew she had become curious about the mystery of being in love with a man.

Seated on a stool, she dried her hair, which Razul Bey had stroked only a short while ago. There had been a kind of tenderness in his touch, just as there had been ruthless candor in his voice when he'd admitted that he would accept only an untouched girl for his bride.

Lorne flung the hair back from her brow, and her blue eyes shone with a touch of tears. He never spared her feelings. He had let her know that she was here in his tent for the sole purpose of amusing him. All she could do was to stay as reserved as possible and not be diminished by what he forced her to feel when he kissed her. Perhaps she had a secret need for affection, and it betrayed her. Anyway, from now on she would be on her guard, even if he swept her off her feet and overwhelmed her with sensual attentions. That was how he behaved with a *kadin*. Razul Bey was a man of strong passions who knew how to arouse any woman he took in his arms.

Lorne felt a tightening of her abdominal muscles as her gaze dwelt on the bed, a low couch piled with fleecy sheepskins. She felt the silk of her slip as it slid down over her skin.... Never before had she felt so aware of herself. She had become aware of her body in relation to a man—how it was made, and how it could be adjusted to the desires of a man, there on those sheepskins, in the dimness of a desert tent.

The imagined scene was devastating, for Lorne could almost see it—Razul Bey's skin blending warm and brown with her white skin, his lips wandering over her from head to toe.

The girls at the convent school had whispered about lovemaking in the dormitory at night. Some of them had yearned for it to happen, while others had dreaded such an intrusion of their privacy. "I'd sooner be a nun!" some had said, Lorne among them.

There was no such hope of that in the tent of the bey.

CHAPTER TEN

THE DRESS WAS the color of jacaranda, the silky fabric glimmering softly about Lorne's slender figure. She had been rather annoyed that Kasha had selected the kind of dresses that would please his lordship, and she had thought of dining with him in her riding trousers.

Instantly, however, she had realized what would happen if she did so. The lord of the desert would remove them, and a potent situation would arise, over which she would have very little control. Overcome by caution, she had put on the silk dress and matching slippers with gemmed heels. The slippers were pretty, but they pinched her toes; her feet weren't quite so narrow as those of a desert girl. The kind of girl who was guarded from men such as Razul Bey...until she married.

Lorne wandered over to the table, where she would eat her first desert supper with the bey. Beside it was the couch, invitingly lit by the cassia-oil lamps.

Every aspect of the *grande tente* was disturbingly intimate. The many carpets that adorned the walls were in a range of Oriental colors and designs, hanging down to meet those underfoot. Here and there on the carpeted floor were kneeling cushions, and on another low table there was a silver-rimmed humidor in readiness for the bey, who enjoyed his smoke after a meal.

Lorne appeared cool in the flower-blue dress, but inwardly she was very far from composed. She wasn't certain how she would react when Razul Bey came to join her in the tent. Above all she wanted to look at her most reserved, as if unaffected by him. The devil mustn't suspect that he had got under her skin and made her aware of her romantic, vulnerable nature.

Images of the desert slid through her mind, of how they had galloped side by side over the undulating sands, until the sun had started to sink. She couldn't deny that the barbaric beauty of sky and sands had stirred her more deeply than when she had ridden alone.

Beneath that brazen sky the sands had seemed to quiver, changing from bronze to gold, from shadowed saffron to shadowed violet. No place on earth could be so fascinating, and Razul Bey had grown up in such surroundings. From boyhood he had absorbed the mystery and danger of those limitless spaces, tawny as a lion's pelt, so fiercely sunlit during the day that the dunes smoked and the rocks cracked. When night fell suddenly, after the riotous sunset, the desert changed its aspect to a brooding kind of beauty. And on those nights when the moon came up, the hyenas howled, and jackals ran in the moonglow.

How could a boy not be magnetized by such a timeless land? How could he stay unaffected by its pagan moon and burning sun?

At last Lorne could understand him a little, though it was no use pretending that she felt any less of a prisoner in his *douar*. She wasn't here of her own free will, and it rankled. It would always do so, because in idolizing freedom himself, he seemed not to care that he took away her right to choose or reject his company.

She knelt on one of the leather cushions and wondered if she would ever have willingly sought the company of such a man. She tried to visualize the two of them in a more civilized situation, and she decided that had he been raised in France he would still have been a force to be reckoned with. Heads would still have turned when he passed by, for he had the supple, fearless-eyed look of a desert man, and that was how Lorne would always see him. No amount of civilized living could ever tame such a man.

Suddenly, with his noiseless tread, Razul Bey entered the tent, pausing just inside to look at Lorne, who still knelt upon the cushion... as if she were his slave girl in waiting.

"God grant me superb indifference," she prayed. But it was not to be.... Every corner of the tent now seemed to hold the aura of the bey, who was clad in a dark silken tunic over *serrouel*, his head uncovered to reveal very black hair, cut low against the nape of his neck. Every inch of him was imposing, and for endless moments Lorne was held motionless by his amber eyes alone.

There was no escape from his eyes.... She saw a slumbering fire in them as he came toward her. She was pitched to an utmost awareness of him, knowing that within seconds he would be close enough to touch her.

"You are a temptress." He took her by the shoulders and drew her upright, until she felt the pressure of his lithe body against her.

"Oh, when have I ever tempted you?" She didn't mean to sound provocative, but the words came out that way.

He slowly ran his eyes over her upraised face, then he stroked his hand over her hair, casually combed and clipped just above her left temple. "What a charming picture you make, yet I half expected you to appear in your riding outfit."

Lorne caught her breath. He seemed to see right through her, and it was disturbing to be his open book, while in return she found him so unreadable.

"Am I right?" he murmured.

"You always seem to think you are, Lord Razul."

"I wonder if you will ever use my name without the title?"

"I doubt it, my lord." Then out of sheer curiosity she asked, "Were you given a French name, as well, in deference to your mother's nationality?"

"Ah, curious about me?" His hands seemed to press her a shade closer to him, so that his firm body could be felt through the fragile silk she was wearing.

"I admit to being a little curious about your mother," she admitted.

"Because of her relationship with my father, eh?" His eyes glittered behind the black veil of his lashes. "Are you one of those who believes that East and West are twain that should never meet?"

"Perhaps—" Lorne looked uncertain.

"A man is still a man, *bint*. A woman still a woman no matter if shades of skin or the rules of Koran and Bible draw a fine distinction between them. Yes, I was given a French name, too, but I have always chosen to be Razul, the son of Hassan Kebîr."

"Won't you tell me your French name?"

"What difference would it make? I wouldn't answer to it."

"Do you dislike your French blood so much, Lord Razul?"

"My choice was made when I was but a child and taken on desert trips by the Lord Hassan. He taught me to be proud of my Eastern heritage, and as I grew into manhood, I had no affinity with the West."

"Yet you read Western books—I've seen them in the bookcases at the palace."

"I attended a military school in southern France, but that doesn't mean that I ever became a Frenchman. No more—" his eyes kindled into a smile "—than you became a nun because you attended a convent school. We are what we are—what we must be."

"You call it fate, but you twisted events to suit your own purpose." She didn't want his smiling eyes to affect her so. His smile was like the tiger's purr, not to be trusted.

"I blew the sands into a storm? I caused your grandfather to fall dead?" His smile became derisive. "Come, my powers aren't that elemental."

"You took advantage of the storm, and of Lion's death." She tried not to remember how his mouth had felt when he kissed her. "You know you did."

"What if I was being protective and you misunderstood me?"

"Protective?" Lorne's eyes searched his face. "Rubbish! You had a score to settle with Lion, and I was the pawn in the game. If you wanted me to believe otherwise, then you shouldn't have said the things you did say about Lion. You could have left me with my illusions. But you chose to hurt me instead."

Perhaps a hint of sadness in her voice, perhaps a shadow in her eyes made him release her, his fingertips traveling down her arm to her hand, which he held briefly. He seemed lost in thought for a moment. Then he took something from his pocket and handed it to Lorne.

She backed away from him, for she could see something expensive, glinting and blue in his fingers. "No—I don't want to take it."

"It seems a pity." He ran his eyes over her dress, then glanced at what he held, a chain of blue scarabs, centered by a moonstone. "It seems made for the dress you are wearing."

"What are you doing?" She backed farther away from him. "Trying to bribe me?"

"Always you give me an argument." In a stride he had caught up with Lorne, and quickly he looped the chain of scarabs about her waist and fastened them. His hands rested on her hips, firmly enough to let her know that the chain was staying where he had put it.

"You must always have your own way, mustn't you?" Lorne stood motionless between his hands, trying not to feel their touch through the fine silk of her dress. "No woman must ever dare to defy you, least of all when you hand out presents. They're payment for being at your beck and call, I suppose? For being your toy, until the fun wears off, and you get bored.''

"You will know soon enough when I am bored." His eyes shifted their amber lights over her face. "I have never in my life met anyone so perverse as you, *ma cherie*. Is this tent not to your liking? Is the desert not a place you have longed to explore? Did you put on such a dress in order not to be noticed by me?''

"It's less revealing than others packed by Kasha."

"There will be other nights," he said, a meaningful look in his eyes. "Tonight, after supper, we are to be entertained. Travelers have camped nearby, and they have with them a dancer and her musicians. Have you ever seen our kind of dancing?''

"Yes, in Bar-Soudi."

"Ah, in a café, no doubt. This will be far more interesting for you, to see a desert girl dance in the firelight. They are taught from childhood and become supple as snakes."

"Perhaps she'll request your company for the night, my lord." Lorne spoke impulsively. "I hope so!"

"By Allah—" In sudden anger he lifted her clear off her feet and then arched her like a bow across his arm. "You are asking for the very thing that you insist you don't want. As I said of you, perverse, with a tongue that runs away with you. You had better be grateful that I am fully adult and not a tempestuous boy, who would sweep you off to his bed this instant and silence those sweet looking lips that spit fire at a man.''

"L-let me down," she gasped. "You're breaking me in half—"

"I'm tempted." He relaxed his hold slightly, then bent his head and took her mouth in a breathless, inescapable kiss. Lorne felt the warmth of their blended bodies, the pressure of his muscles, the inescapable strength. Once again in his arms she was forced to face her own vulnerability. His kiss was a flame that swept through her and made ashes of her inhibitions. The exquisite tip of the flame made her quiver from head to heel, and with a will of their own, her hands reached for his black hair, and her fingers buried themselves in its thickness.

Oh, it was too cruel of the fates to make him so exciting to touch—and how could she believe him heartless anymore, when his heart beat to be felt, there against her own?

With a sensuous slowness, his lips drew away from hers, and it was with the effort of a dream-held sleeper that Lorne slowly opened her eyes to meet his.

She stared at the burnt-gold of his face, the skin close-grained over the strong, proud bones. She couldn't make a sound, as if bound by a spell she didn't wish to break. "You are going to tell me the thoughts that went through your head just now." He spoke in her ear, a sound like sandy velvet. "If you hated me then, you will hate me forever."

"Will you care . . . ?" The words were barely audible, for his closeness destroyed her will to resist him. The touch of him tangled her thoughts; they were incapable of being sorted out so that she could give him a straight answer. Hate? Was it possible to hate a man whose body seemed to become part of her own when they were close . . . close like this?

"I am waiting," he warned. "I want to know what you were thinking when we kissed."

"I—I wasn't thinking—"

"Don't lie to me." His eyes smoldered, like the desert under a brazen sun. "Come, stop being childish and be honest with me. Or shall I read your eyes? Shall I look into the mirror of your pupils and see—ah, but I see only myself. There I am in the eyes of the Desirée girl, the Lord Razul Etienne Kebîr."

Etienne! The name curiously shook Lorne. Was she right in believing that Razul Bey's mother had given him the name of the Frenchman, lover and husband, who had perished in the desert? Wouldn't she do the same, if she loved a man?

"Away with you, then." The bey released her from his arms, only a matter of moments before Abdul entered the tent with their supper on a large silver tray. Lorne saw him brush a hand over his hair, and then there wasn't a sign that they had kissed with such abandon. Like the tiger, she thought, his senses attuned to the slightest sound, to the slightest shift of mood.

"Supper smells delicious," she said in French to Abdul, a man who was less stern-faced than the armed guards. He gave her a gratified look. He would now and again converse with Lorne, and sometimes look at her as if he felt *sympathique*.

"Come and eat your delicious supper," Razul Bey ordered, but Lorne took her time approaching the couch where the table was being laid with their meal. Close to him again, she would be robbed of her perspective. She would be sensitized to every movement of his supple body. She would watch his brown hands as he ate his food in the Eastern way.

"I thought you were hungry." His eyes mocked her slow approach. "Do you want the *couscous* to go cold?"

Lorne sat down without replying, doing her best to look as if she were dining in a *café l'Arabe* with a total stranger. When he seated himself beside her, she spread her serviette carefully across her knees and watched Abdul as he served the first course. This was a vegetable broth served with hunks of brown bread, and so ambrosial that Lorne cleared her soup bowl with the alacrity of a navvy who had been laying bricks all day.

Razul Bey didn't say a word, but Lorne heard him laugh softly to himself. Their *couscous* was a mound of saffron-tinted rice served with lamb cutlets and kidney. Butter-tossed onions, peas and carrots were laid on side plates. The gravy was brown and aromatic, and Abdul no longer lingered, retreating in his quiet way through the tent flap.

"Can you roll a rice ball in your fingers yet?"

"Not the way you can." Lorne, as usual, was mesmerized by the dexterity with which he ate his food. He made eating with his fingers look easy and not in the least impolite.

"Make an attempt. Here in the desert you must become accustomed to our ways—which may include riding a camel."

"Are you serious?" She couldn't stop herself from looking at him.

"About the rice balls?"

"No, about the camel—am I really going to be taught to ride one?"

"If the notion appeals to you." He gave her a sardonic look and ate buttered peas by rolling them in rice. "I have it in mind to be your tutor, and the first lesson is that you stop being inhibited by English prudery. There's a special kind of satisfaction in eating with the fingers—they are, you know, one of the most sensitive zones of the body, especially so when they meet lips and tongue in the act of eating. Watch me and try to emulate me."

Lorne strove to ignore the note of suggestiveness in his remark. "I don't think I'm a prude because I prefer to eat the English way."

"You are a long way from the cool green fields of England. You are in El Karah, and it's my wish that you learn our ways."

"What if it's my wish to remain exactly as I am?" She gave him a defiant look.

"I am the Lord Razul." He leaned toward her and took away the spoon with which she was eating her *couscous*. "And my wishes take precedence over yours. Now do as you are told, *bint*. Roll that piece of kidney in rice—no, not too much at a time or the food will spill from your fingers. There, now quickly toss the rice ball into your mouth."

Miraculously the food entered her mouth, and the contact with her fingertips was curiously pleasant and seemed to add to the taste of the food. It was a sensuous way of eating, but Lorne wasn't going to admit that to the bey, who probably guessed, anyway.

"Now lift a cutlet in your fingers and chew the meat from the bone. Don't give me that wide-eyed look. Do as you are told. Discover that there are enjoyments you never dreamed about, and stop feeling guilty whenever something gives you a sense of pleasure. We wouldn't have our senses if they weren't meant to be enjoyed. We would be figures of clay, *mon amour*."

A smile played about in his eyes as he watched Lorne taking rather self-conscious bites out of the lamb cutlet that she held in her fingers.

"Our eyes would have the vacant gaze of statues," he went on. "Our lips would always be sealed. Our ears would never respond to music or the song of a bird. We would never know how delectable food can smell, nor find haunting the scent of flowers in a walled garden after a fall of rain. We would possess no sense of touch, nor taste. We would feel none of the emotions that make life exciting. No angers, therefore no calms. No hates, therefore no loves. No pains, therefore no pleasures."

He paused, his eyes intent upon Lorne. "The meat tastes good, eh, when you eat it straight off the bone."

She had to agree with him; it did seem the more natural way to eat, especially when dining in the tent of a Bey. But how shocked the nuns would be if they could see her popping carrots and peas in her mouth without using cutlery. Discipline and decorum had been all important—the poor, dear nuns had tried their hardest to suppress their pupil's natural inclinations.

Lorne was at a loss to know what was best for girls when they were growing up, into a world that was still the domain of the male. "You must behave properly" had been a constant warning. "Modesty, prudence and truth are the marks of a lady. Immodesty, indiscretion and impudence are the telltale signs of a wanton."

Some of the girls had giggled together over what it meant to be wanton. They had looked it up in the dictionary and relished such words as capricious, reckless and amorous.

As Lorne wiped her fingers on her serviette, she gave the man at her side a suspicious look. What was he trying to do? Was he trying to make her react like an Eastern girl?

Abdul took away the *couscous* dish and returned with a large bowl of mixed fruits. A fresh pot of coffee was brought in, along with a selection of nuts and sweets. "We are looking forward to the dancing." Razul Bey spoke to his manservant in French so Lorne could understand him. "The *lel-lah* has never seen a real desert dancer, so it will be interesting for her, eh?"

"They are—strange women." Abdul poured the coffee and gave Lorne one of his questing looks.

"What Abdul is inferring—" the bey watched Lorne as he stirred his coffee "—is that these women are in the oldest profession in the world. They start young, amass a fortune and then return to their tribe to become respected wives and mothers. You comprehend?"

Lorne flushed as she remembered what she had said to him about the dancer inviting his attentions. "I'm not quite a child," she rejoined.

"In some matters, *bint*, you are a pure innocent."

Lorne held back her reply until Abdul had left the tent, "You say that, Lord Razul, but your intentions toward me aren't in the least pure, or innocent."

"What are my intentions, pray?" He was studying the fruit bowl, beside which lay a silver knife with a pointed blade, glistening and sharp.

Lorne's gaze was on the knife as she sipped her coffee. "You didn't bring me here out of friendship, did you?"

"Did I not?" His lean fingers selected a large and luscious fig.

"Don't give me one of your veiled looks, Razul Bey. You and I could never be friends."

"Never is a long, long time, Lorne *chérie*." Smiling to himself, he divided the fig and pushed a piece between Lorne's lips before she could protest. "To share a fig is to make harmony. So eat and enjoy, and stop making of your brain a treadmill on which your thoughts go round and round."

With the piece of fig in her mouth, Lorne was obliged to consume it. Quite delicious, of course, but unsettling because of the way he watched her as he ate his own portion.

"It was surely the fig tree that grew in the garden of Eden," he said, absolutely at his ease as he lounged beside her. "A much more evocative fruit than the homely apple, don't you agree? An enticing and mysterious fruit."

"No doubt the serpent would have selected it rather than the apple," Lorne agreed, dabbing her lips and trying to look remote, which wasn't easy on account of Razul Bey's nearness, so masculine, so vital and all-knowing. If she made an attempt to remove herself, he might pull her down into his arms, and Lorne no longer trusted herself when she felt his warm brown skin touching hers. Even to think of it was to feel a strange, melting weakness, as if some second self, some hidden creature, was taking her over and making her a slave to feelings she couldn't fight—not when he touched her.

She sat there rigidly, fearing the slightest movement of his hand. Every single nerve reacted when he reached for the humidor and selected one of his thin cigars. The dark leaf wrapping crackled in his fingers. Then the lighter flared, and the blue smoke drifted into the lamplit air.

"Don't you care for sweets?" he asked. "That Turkish delight looks as if it would melt in the mouth. Do eat some. Otherwise, Abdul will be disappointed. He has served it solely on your account, for he knows my preferences."

"Has he been with you a long time?" Solely to please Abdul, she selected a piece of the confection. She nibbled, the bey smoked, and outside the tent there was the throb of drums and the wailing of a flute. It was a moment of such mystery and strangeness, that Lorne's heart gave a throb. This was reality, not a dream. She was here in the tent of a desert chief. He sat beside her in Eastern clothing, his face a brooding sculpture in the smoke-tinged lamplight.

"Does it surprise you," he asked, "that those in my service stay with me a long time? Am I such a monster in your eyes?"

"You are served by people of your own sort, who understand your ways. If your ways seem strange to me, surely that is understandable, Lord Razul?"

"We have a saying, *mon amie*." Smoke curled from his lips. "All women are fundamentally one woman, and her name is Eve."

"Have all men one name, that of Adam?"

"Possibly. He set the pattern, did he not? He allowed himself to be enticed, and he said to Allah, 'The woman thou gavest to be with me, she gave me of the tree, and I did eat.' "

"So forever and forever Eve is to blame for everything?"

He smoked in silence for several moments, and the throbbing drums out there in the firelight were like the heartbeats of a runner, pounding against tautly drawn skin. "Yes," Razul Bey said at last. "I believe there is a beckoning in a woman's eyes, which a man is doomed to follow, not always to felicity, of course."

"That's a very arrogant statement, my lord."

"Really? I thought it was a rather profound one, but a girl such as yourself would be unlikely to know of the subtleties, the cruelties and the ecstasies that take place between a man and a woman when they become involved. Perhaps you would like to believe that offspring pop out of a pod that grows under the shade of a tree. Yes, I look at you, Lorne *chérie*, and I see the wish in your eyes that love was closer to the heavens than the earth."

"I never give love a thought," she rejoined. "I've better things to think about."

"Such as getting out of my clutches, eh?" His eyes glimmered through the smoke of his cigar. "Do take your gaze off that fruit knife—I really don't fancy a stab in the heart. I have my work to do. I have my people to consider."

"It's a pity you didn't consider them when you took me into your clutches."

He rocked his hand in a very Eastern gesture. "Would you have come to El Karah if I had suggested it to you that morning when we confronted each other, and the wind howled as if it were a demon trying to get into the house?"

Lorne looked startled, for that's how she had thought of the wind as it whined and rattled the shutters. Her thoughts fled backward to that morning, following a night of misery and loneliness. What had Razul Kebîr seen when he looked at her? Was she mistaken about him? Had he seen a lonely, helpless girl who needed some care and attention?

Abruptly her eyes filled with tears, but she strove not to let them fall, forcing them back instead.

"Come, we must go and watch the dancing girl." The bey swung to his feet and extended a hand to Lorne—lean, brown, and too bewildering if it should touch her.

"Y-you go ahead." She spoke in a rather stifled voice. "I need to tidy myself."

"As you wish." He leaned down to stub his cigar, and in the same movement he removed the knife, with its wickedly shining blade.

Lorne caught her breath, and something of a very disturbing nature was in the very air as their eyes met. Then she watched in silence as he left the tent, carrying the knife. Watched as the flap fell into place behind his tall figure. Oh yes, there had been a time when she would have plunged a knife into him, but somehow the will to wound him had lost its sharp edge.

There, in the veiled-off area of the tent, Lorne hovered and hesitated. She wished she could enjoy what he was thinking, that she despised him enough to knife him.

As she tidied her hair with the tortoiseshell comb, she met her gaze in the painted mirror. Her eyes seemed shadowed by more than the tears she had very nearly cried, and her lips were somehow poised on a question that had no simple answer. She attempted to see herself as a man would see her. She touched her hair as Razul Bey had sometimes touched it, feeling its texture and the way it framed her face.

Hesitantly, curiously, she allowed her fingers to trail against the smoothness of her neck, and with a sudden rush of feeling she realized that she wanted the touch of the lean brown fingers that had picked up the knife, lying there between them like a symbol of all the differences that separated them.

A desert of difference lay between them. Lion had sometimes talked about the growing enmity between the various countries, the flare-ups that led to bloodshed, the hatreds that fed on rebellion and the age-old distrust of foreigners.

Lorne slowly wrapped herself in a cloak, then went outside into the leaping firelight, which illumed her figure as she went to sit beside Razul Bey on a rug that had been spread on the sands. Something in her expression fixed his eyes upon her face, but when the drumbeats quickened, he looked away, in the direction of a pagan figure, painted and glittering with jewelry, anklets of tiny golden bells sounding her approach, which was made on bare and hennaed feet, like a tigress padding in, out of the darkness beyond the ring of fires.

Tulle to her ankles hung from a beaded girdle, slung around the curve of her hips. There were chains of beads against the transparent tulle across her bosom. A collar of beads encircled her throat, and there were more of them fixed in her cascading black hair. Patterns of henna adorned her hands, and bracelets hung on her arms.

There, in the firelight, she was a barbaric figure, her arching eyebrows joined above her kohl-dusted eyes. As the flute began its wailing, she began to dance, her bell anklets clinking and jingling as she arched her sinuous body to the music. She was the embodiment of the harem dancer imagined by Lorne, her undulating hips and arms beckoning men into her embrace.

Tentatively Lorne slid her glance to the bey, and she watched him and wondered what lay beyond the inscrutability of his fire-bronzed face. Did the tigress body of the dancer excite his imagination? Was Lorne, the *roumia*, quite forgotten when he watched a girl of the desert performing a dance whose sensual enticements were plain to see?

The throb of the drums was like a heart beating with wild longings. The strange flute notes were like cries, rising and falling in the night. And, silently, the circle of men watched this courtesan of the deep and sultry heart of the desert, eyes gleaming in the firelight as she arched her body like a bow, and her bracelets slid like golden fire down her arms to her hennaed hands. She stayed in that position for interminable moments, and her body seemed to undulate like a snake shedding its skin.

When she leaped suddenly to her feet, Lorne couldn't suppress a gasp. Then, like a tigress, she sprang toward the Lord Razul, and Lorne saw a fanatical gleam in the almond-shaped eyes. A thrill of fear ran through Lorne. She knew something awful was about to happen—some nightmare was about to be repeated.

"Razul—!"

Even as Lorne cried out his name, steel flew from his fingers, and the sharp blade buried itself among the golden beads that hung around the dancer's neck. As she toppled, something fell from her fingers and lay gleaming in the light of the fires. A moment more, and she would have pulled the trigger of the gun and shot the bey in the heart. Only a fraction of time lay between nightmare and the sudden silence, abruptly broken as men leaped to their feet.

As commotion swept the *douar*, Lorne was hustled by Razul Bey into his tent. "Stay here!" His gaze impelled her, and his face was darkly grim. "So the knife was meant for a throat, eh?"

Lorne clutched at him, and her face was so white that her eyes held him with their blueness. "Why?" she whispered. "Because of me, Razul?"

"I have to find out the reason. Right now we can't talk. Stay in here. You will be safe with two of my guards posted outside." His hands tightened on her, then let go. "So, at last you say my name. Such irony should make me smile, *mon ange*."

She watched him as he strode frowning from the tent. She heard him speak outside, and his Arabic sounded threatening, as if he were giving strict orders with regard to her safety. A wave of reaction swept over her, and she sank to a floor cushion and buried her face in her hands.

Her mind was raw with images—if the gun had been fired it would have been Razul Bey who lay in his blood on the sand.

The horror of the intention was almost more than Lorne could stand, especially if she was the cause. Mercifully, the dancer's reflexes had been a fraction slower than the bey's, and Lorne winced at the memory of the flying steel, so lethally directed at the dancer.

So this at last was the reality of the desert, where the passions were as fierce and ruthless as the burning sun. Where hatred could hide behind a veil and take its revenge in ways not to be imagined, unless witnessed.

Lorne huddled into her cloak. What if Razul wanted to send her away? Those events, which Lion had often talked about, were dividing the East, and tonight her life had been touched by them, uncovering a truth she could no longer evade. At some unsuspected moment, perhaps as they rode in the desert, Razul Kebîr had found his way into her heart, and only a while ago she had been terrified of losing him.

Lorne drew a shuddering sigh and listened to the activity beyond the walls of the tent. She wanted to be part of it. Alone like this, she was at the mercy of too many thoughts, vivid as a montage in desert colors... bangles and beads, streaming with blood, and the look of agony in almond-shaped eyes ringed with kohl dust.

Her mind seethed with images she couldn't seem to blot out. They slid in sequence through her mind, like the memory of a nightmare. If Razul Bey had not taken the knife with him—but it was not to be imagined, that strong body without its proud heartbeat.

With a look of irony in his eyes, Razul had carried the knife from the tent, believing she would use it on him. Instead, it had saved his life, a strange reinforcement of the Eastern belief that all things were written in the sand.

What would now happen to their strange relationship, with all its conflict and all its fatal charm? Would the bey feel compelled to send her away, out of his life, the European woman with whom he had chosen to share his tent? Whatever the fun in the game he had played with her, that fun had turned into something more dangerous. They were caught now in the crosscurrents of a storm that wouldn't die so easily as the sirocco when its fury was spent.

Confused and shaky, Lorne tried to reason it out. There was no way she could push from her mind the thought that love didn't dictate the actions of Razul Bey, not where she was concerned. Whatever her appeal to him, she had now become a liability and a danger to his position among his people. He was proud of that position, and his protection of it would seem to exclude her.

A desolate feeling swept over Lorne, something she had never expected to feel in relation to the bey. She was relieved when Abdul came in, carrying a pot of coffee.

"Abdul, what's happening?" She had to enquire, but her eyes were shaded by her fear of being told.

"The things that have to happen, *lel-lah*." He poured the coffee for her and added brown sugar and cream. He handed her the cup, and she took it gratefully. The fragrance filled her nostrils, and her lips warmed themselves at the rim. When she swallowed some of the coffee, her throat reacted with a touch of pain—the pain of emotions that she was holding in check.

"He'll be ruthless, won't he, Abdul?"

Razul Bey's manservant spread his hands in a significant gesture. "How else does a man deal with fanatics, *lel-lah*? Death means nothing to them. Their sole aim is to stir up rebellion. This is spreading across the desert like the sands driven by a scorching wind."

Lorne's eyes darkened with pain. "Why are people such fools? Why do they quarrel? Why do they seek to impose their opinions on others? Why is love such a difficult thing for us to accept?"

"Love is a commitment, *lel-lah*."

"A commitment," she murmured.

"And so is hatred."

Lorne shuddered, for it was a word she had used in dealing with Razul Bey. She had thrown it in his face and sworn she would hate him forever. But she hadn't known the true meaning of hatred until tonight, when the dancer had sprung at him with deadly intent.

"Will we return to the palace?" she asked.

Abdul inclined his white-turbaned head. "My Lord Razul has already given orders for the tents to be taken down in the early morning."

"I see."

Lorne saw all too clearly what would happen when they arrived at the palace. She was now caught up in a rebellion that was being driven across the sands as the winds had been driven across L'Oasis, leaving death and destruction in their wake, changing for always the destiny of the girl who had stood on the gallery, shaking with nerves after a night of lonely terror.

Always the arguments and the wars seemed to be over territory... Lorne remembered vividly how Razul Bey had spoken about Lion, about the way her grandfather had held on to something that wasn't really his. The bey had come to the plantation in order to take back what belonged to him. It all came back to her—that morning of dust and heat, and the drifting smoke of the burning house as he rode away with her, holding her on the saddlebow of his camel.

Tomorrow the camels would return with their riders to the palace, and, for possibly the last time, Lorne would ride the proud chestnut at the bey's side.

She came out of her reverie to find herself once more alone in the big tent with its barbaric trappings. Slowly she gazed around her, and her gaze dwelt on the couch where she and Razul Bey had shared a *couscous*. Then he had been saying to her: "I'll teach you to be a girl of the East."

But she wasn't of the East. She was the *femme blonde*, and the time had come for Razul Bey to set her free from the captivity she had despised—the captivity she had fought against, until this moment of truth.

She had thought never to face such heart-shocking truth, and she didn't know how to conceal it as the bey strode suddenly into the tent.

"You look," he said, "the way you looked that first morning of our lives."

"I've been thinking of that morning—do you want cof
fee, my lord? Abdul hasn't long brought it in."

"Coffee would be most acceptable." He stretched out or
the couch as he spoke, and when Lorne brought the brim
ming cup to him, she saw what she had rarely seen in hi
amber eyes, a look of weariness and a shadow of pain.

"Merci, mon amie." As he accepted the cup, their eye
met. "Will you sit beside me?"

"If it's what you would like?"

"What I would like—" he took a long pull at the coffe
"—is perhaps something I shouldn't mention."

Lorne sat tensely at his side, and something in he
brimmed with the need to know what he wanted. "Tell me,'
she said.

He shook his head. "There is a time to be foolish and a
time to be wise, and we both know that I must be wise fo
both of us. Wise for us, *mon ange*, wise for my people."

"I see." Lorne lowered her gaze, her hands clenched to
gether in her lap, as if badly in need of something to cling to
"Did you find out why that girl tried to—to kill you?"

"Not as yet, but I will certainly find out. So you wer
concerned for me, eh?"

Lorne shuddered visibly. "It was terrible—I can still hea
the whack of the knife—I can still see the blood."

"The sands have soaked up a lot of blood in their time.'

"I'm so glad, Razul that it wasn't your blood."

"Are you?"

"Yes."

"There was a time when you would have rejoiced in seein;
me dead."

"I know—" She was glad that her hair veiled her expres
sion, for her very skin had tightened across the bones of he
face, as if in that moment she grew out of the skin of the gir
into the body of the woman.

"I found out differently—tonight," she said.

Silence hung on the air, then she heard him place the coffee cup on the table, and she felt him draw closer to her, a closeness she no longer shrank from.

"You don't wish me in paradise?" he murmured.

The note of irony in his voice made her look at him to see what was in his eyes. She caught her breath and felt the faintness that had not assailed her out there in the firelight, the thud of the drums warming up to a deadly climax. His eyes smoldered—they held all the passions of the desert, savage and dangerous . . . beguiling and beckoning.

"Tomorrow—" she moistened her lips "—are you going to send me away?"

"Do you want to go?"

"No—no, my lord." Her hands sprang of their own volition, around his neck in a clasp like that of someone drowning. She drew down his head, and she kissed him with all the passion she had held in check. Over and over again she kissed him, and like some supple, tawny tiger in a mood of compliance, Razul Bey half closed his eyes as Lorne's lips traveled over his face and found the warm column of his neck.

"You are taking a grave risk," he murmured.

"The risk has always been there." Her lips fondled his earlobe and found it quite hot, as if it were the barometer of his emotions. "There hasn't been a day or a night when I've felt really safe with you, my lord."

"And now you are feeling brave, eh? What has made you brave, I wonder? The realization that I'm not immune from having my heart ripped out?"

She hugged him to her and felt the beating of his heart, like a reassurance that tonight they were together, and the dawn seemed far away.

"Did Lion really offer me," she asked, "like the sacrificial lamb?"

"I am afraid he did, *mon ange*."

"And what did you really say to him?"

"I said the words in my own language, and they aren't repeatable."

"You said them that night—that night when I saw you go storming out of the house?"

"Were you in hiding, watching me?"

"Yes." She remembered how she had stood in an alcove of the shadowy hall and watched the bey stride past in his great cloak, his face as detailed and as seemingly cruel as a golden mask on a tomb.

Lorne touched his face and traced her fingers over the features that were so Eastern, so much the outward sign of all that could separate them. "Yet you took me to El Karah," she said softly. "Was it really because I called you a dog?"

"Yes, it probably was."

"You never lie, do you, Razul?"

"Not if I can help it."

"Then tell me what you're going to do with me."

They both knew what she wanted from him, but he evaded the answer as he lifted her into his arms. "I'm going to do what I came to the desert to do." His eyes looked down into hers, and Lorne could see there was no stopping him, even if she had wanted him to stop. She made no demur as he carried her to the veiled area of the tent and stepped through to where the bed awaited them.

He laid her down on the sheepskins and unclasped the belt of scarabs that he had hung about her waist. It fell gleaming to the carpet, blue as Lorne's eyes, as she felt the brown hands of Razul Bey undressing her.

The sharing of danger had heightened their need of each other, and Lorne luxuriated beneath his touch. The inhibitions were gone, and all that mattered was that Razul take her for his own.

He flung off his own clothing, and for the first time, her body felt the bare warmth of his skin, the brush of dark hair, the seeking thrust of him. She responded with eager desire for him, her flesh and nerves quivering to the potent feel of him. She was his, and he was hers.

Even the pain was welcome because he caused it, and then came the pleasure, throbbing and streaming through her body, to its utmost reaches. Their movements were sweet-hot, silken, and his breath mingled with hers in kisses that were tempestuous and everywhere. Her hair was tossed gold across the pillows as she discovered with Razul just how loving and giving she could be with a man. Lorne's willingness, at last, was a thing of wonder to both of them.

They loved through the night with a passion bright as a flame, and whatever was written in the sands was written. They had no way of knowing, not beyond tonight and its passionate needs. Tonight was only the beginning. . . .

VIOLET WINSPEAR, who calls herself a true Cockney, born within sound of London's Bow Bells, began inventing stories while still at school, and at fourteen began work at a book bindery. Because she realized that people need an escape from life's harsh realities, she began writing romances. Her first Romance was published in 1961, her first Presents appeared in 1973. She is one of the select group of authors who have produced more than fifty Harlequins.

Books by Violet Winspear

HARLEQUIN PRESENTS

492—NO MAN OF HER OWN
566—THE MAN SHE MARRIED
718—BY LOVE BEWITCHED
734—BRIDE'S LACE
854—SUN LORD'S WOMAN

HARLEQUIN ROMANCE

1616—THE PAGAN ISLAND
1637—THE SILVER SLAVE
1658—DEAR PURITAN
1680—RAPTURE OF THE DESERT
2682—SECRET FIRE

HARLEQUIN SIGNATURE EDITION

THE HONEYMOON

Can you keep a secret?

You can keep this one plus 4 free novels

Harlequin Presents

Coming Next Month